THE TEMPTATION OF TORILLA

Torilla heard voices drawing near and she braced herself for a contact with the Marquis—a man whose reputation for extravagance and cruelty terrified her.

"Here is Gallen, Torilla, and now you can meet him," she heard her cousin say.

With an effort Torilla raised her eyes. Then her heart did a double somersault in her breast and the whole room seemed to whirl around her.

Torilla recognized the notorious Marquis of Havingham as none other than the handsome stranger who had saved her from peril the night of her stagecoach accident!

Bantam Books by Barbara Cartland
Ask your bookseller for the books you have missed

Barbara Cartland's Library of Love

Barbara Cartland
The Temptation of Torilla

BANTAM BOOKS
TORONTO · NEW YORK · LONDON

THE TEMPTATION OF TORILLA
A Bantam Book | September 1977

ISBN 0–553–11271–6

Published simultaneously in the United States and Canada

Bantam Books are published by Bantam Books, Inc. Its trade-
mark, consisting of the words "Bantam Books" and the por-
trayal of a bantam, is registered in the United States Patent
Office and in other countries. Marca Registrada. Bantam
Books, Inc., 666 Fifth Avenue, New York, New York 10019.

Author's Note

It was not until 1842 that the first report by the Children's Employment Commission awoke the conscience of the country. The conditions in the coal mines described in this novel are all from the report.

Safety devices were slow in being introduced. John Buddle's Air-Pump in 1807, the Davy-lamp in 1816, then John Martin's Air Lock and Fan was not in use until 1835.

What struck the Victorians more than the danger of explosion was that girls as well as boys were employed together. Naked to the waist with chains between their legs, the future mothers of Englishmen crawled on all fours down tunnels under the earth, drawing gigantic burdens.

Women by the age of thirty were old and infirm cripples. Such labour was often accompanied by debauchery and terrible cruelty.

When Lord Ashley a month after the report introduced a Bill to exclude all women and girls from the pits, and boys under thirteen, he was acclaimed a national hero.

Chapter One

1816

The Dowager Marchioness of Havingham picked up a glass of madeira as she said:

"The doctors have forbidden me to touch alcohol, but I must celebrate your arrival, dearest."

"Have they done you any good, Mama?"

The Marquis as he asked the question had a note of anxiety in his voice which did not escape his mother's ear.

She was used to the lazy, languid tones which were fashionable amongst the Bucks and Dandies who surrounded the Prince Regent.

She disliked, although she was far too wise to say so, the manner they had of drawling their words and looking at the world from under drooping, supercilious eye-lids.

"I think the water—nasty as it is—has helped to relieve the pain," she replied, "but I find Harrogate very dull, and quite frankly, I am longing to return home."

"Then I have brought you a very good excuse to leave," the Marquis said.

As his mother looked up at him enquiringly, he

rose from the chair on which he had been sitting to stand with his back to the fireplace.

The suite in which the Dowager Marchioness was ensconced in the best and most expensive Hotel in Harrogate was quite pleasant, and the Marquis noted that she had brought to the somewhat austere furnishings of the Sitting-Room many touches that were peculiarly her own.

There was both a portrait in oils and a miniature of himself arranged on one of the side-tables and there were many vases of hot-house flowers—he could never imagine his mother without them.

There were soft cushions which decorated the sombre damask chairs, and most important of all there were her two little King Charles spaniels, who had greeted him effusively on his arrival.

"You are quite cosy here," he said, as if it suddenly struck him that even an Hotel could have some points to it.

"Quite," the Dowager Marchioness replied briefly. "Now tell me, Gallen, what you have come to tell me; for I am quite certain, my dearest, you have not made this long journey just to see if I am comfortable."

As she spoke the Dowager's eyes rested on her son admiringly.

There was no-one, she thought, who could look so handsome, and while being so exquisitely dressed could yet remain overwhelmingly masculine.

The Marquis's clothes fitted his broad shoulders and accentuated his narrow hips, but in fact, since he was so athletic, he was the despair of his tailors.

It was not fashionable to have strong, rippling muscles under the superfine whipcord coats.

But the Marquis was noted as an exceptionally fine pugilist in Gentleman Jackson's Rooms in Bond Street, just as with the rapier he found it hard to find anyone good enough to give him a match.

Combined with this, he was the outstanding Corinthian among his contemporaries, and the younger

Bucks and Blades envied him his expertise with his horses and strove ineffectually to emulate the manner in which he tied his cravats.

And if to the world, or rather the *Beau Monde,* the Marquis appeared indifferent, cynical, and autocratic, his mother knew that where she was concerned he could be considerate, kind, and occasionally surprisingly affectionate.

She knew, therefore, that he spoke the truth when the Marquis said:

"If I thought you really desired my company, Mama, I would come to Harrogate or anywhere else to please you."

"You know I would not impose on you to such an extent," the Dowager Marchioness replied fondly. "But tell me why you have come."

There was a little pause before the Marquis said, drawling his words:

"I have decided to get married."

"Gallen!"

The word was a startled exclamation and now the Dowager Marchioness put down her glass of madeira in case she should spill it.

She clasped her hands together, and raising her eyes to her son's face she asked:

"Do you really mean it? After all these years, you have met someone you really wish to make your wife?"

"I have decided to marry, Mama, because, as you well know, I must have an heir," the Marquis replied. "I also require a wife who is well bred and will not bore me to distraction."

"Whom have you chosen?"

"I have offered for Lady Beryl Fern," the Marquis answered, "and as I did not wish you to read without warning of the engagement in the *Gazette,* I ordered both Beryl and her father not to breathe a word of our intentions until you had been informed."

"Lady Beryl Fern," the Dowager Marchioness said slowly. "But of course I have heard of her."

"She is undoubtedly the most beautiful girl in England," the Marquis explained. "She has been acclaimed since she first burst upon the Social World, and the Prince himself christened her 'the Incomparable' before the experts in the Clubs of St. James's got round to doing so."

There was an undeniably mocking note in the Marquis's voice and his mother looked at him sharply before she said:

"What is she like, Gallen?"

Again there was a little pause before the Marquis replied:

"She enjoys gaiety, as I do, and is the life and soul of every party she attends. She will certainly embellish the Reception Rooms at Havingham House and the Castle, besides doing full justice to that Aladdin's Cave of jewels which you so seldom wear."

"That is not what I asked you, dearest," the Dowager Marchioness said in a low voice.

The Marquis walked with the grace that was peculiarly his own from the hearth-rug to the window, to stand with his back to her, looking out at the trees which so far north were only just showing the green buds of spring.

"What else do you want to know, Mama?" he asked after a moment.

"You know full well what I want to hear," his mother replied. "Are you in love?"

There was silence until the Marquis replied:

"I am thirty-three, Mama, and I am past the pulsating emotions of a love-sick boy."

"Then you are only marrying to beget an heir."

He could hardly hear the words, and yet they had been said.

"I can think of no better reason for taking on a wife," the Marquis said almost defiantly.

"But I would wish you to fall in love."

"As I have already said, I am too old for such nonsense."

"It is not nonsense, Gallen. Your father and I were divinely happy together, and I have prayed that you would know the happiness we found in each other for so many years before he was taken from me."

"They do not make girls like you today, Mama."

The Dowager Marchioness sighed.

"Your father told me that the first moment he saw me at the High Sheriff's garden-party, of all unlikely places, he thought I was enveloped by a white light."

"Papa said that to me, too," the Marquis interposed.

"I did not notice him until he was introduced," his mother went on, her voice very soft as she looked back into the past, "but when he touched my hand something very strange happened."

Her words seemed to vibrate as she said:

"I fell in love at that instant! I knew he was the man of my dreams, the man I had always believed was somewhere in the world, if I could only find him."

"You were very lucky, Mama."

"It was not luck," the Dowager Marchioness contradicted, "it was fate. Although your father's parents were trying to arrange an alliance for him with the Duke of Newcastle's daughter, we knew that nothing mattered except that we should be together for the rest of our lives."

The Marquis moved a little restlessly.

He had heard all this before and it always disturbed him when his mother spoke of his father.

They had loved each other so deeply, so overwhelmingly, that he thought, looking back on his childhood, that everything had been tinged with the aura of their happiness.

Their only sorrow had been that they only had one child—himself—and because he loved his mother he tried to look after her and protect her after his father died.

She did not have to tell him what being in love

as his parents had been could mean: he had seen it with his own eyes. But he knew quite positively that it would never happen to him.

Aloud he said:

"Times have changed, Mama, and love, except where the Prince Regent is concerned, has ceased to be fashionable."

"Love! You cannot speak of his Royal Highness and love in the same breath," the Dowager Marchioness said scornfully. "Look at the way he has treated that poor Mrs. Fitzherbert, and I have always been convinced that they were really married. As for that stupid, flirtatious Lady Hereford, I cannot bear the woman!"

The Marquis laughed.

"He sets the example for all of us, Mama, so you can hardly expect me to find idyllic love at Carlton House."

"And you have decided quite cold-bloodedly to marry Lady Beryl."

"We shall deal well together, Mama," the Marquis replied. "We talk the same language, we have the same friends, and if after we have been married a little while we each go our own ways it will be done with circumspection. There will be no scandal, and any differences between us will be settled amicably."

The Dowager Marchioness did not speak. There was an expression in her eyes of such unhappiness that her son crossed to her side and took one of her hands in his.

"You are not to worry about me, Mama," he said. "It is everything that I wish, and there is no reason why Beryl and I should not produce half-a-dozen robust grandchildren, which I know will give you pleasure."

The Dowager Marchioness's thin blue-veined hand, with several of its knuckles inflamed with arthritis, rested in her son's warm one.

"Your father and I always wanted the best for

you, Gallen, but this, as you must be honest enough to admit, is second best."

"You are still judging my life by yours, Mama," the Marquis said. "I am content, and one cannot ask for more."

"I can, and I do," his mother replied.

Her fingers tightened on his.

"You are not still . . . thinking of that . . . girl who treated you so . . . badly?"

Her voice sounded hesitant, as if she was afraid of offending him, but the Marquis laughed quite unaffectedly.

"No, indeed, Mama. I am not such a ninny as to carry wounds of that sort. I was only a beardless youth at the time, and one's first love-affair, is always over-emotional."

He released his mother's hand, and walking back to the mantelpiece to stare down at the flames leaping high over the logs he did not see the expression on his mother's face or realise that she did not believe him, and her eyes were suddenly full of tears.

It had all happened, as the Marquis had said, a long time ago. He had been twenty-one at the time.

The girl with whom he had fallen in love had been very beautiful and very spoilt. He had adored her in an idealistic manner which she was incapable of understanding.

His mother knew that he had laid his heart and soul at her feet, but she had stamped on them and married a Duke because he had a higher title and at the time a great deal more money.

The Dowager Marchioness thought she would never forget the expression on her son's face when he had come home.

He had not spoken of what had happened, for that would have been impossible for him, but he had wanted to hide himself away so that the world would not know how deeply he had been wounded.

From that moment, she thought now, he had

changed from a happy, laughing, carefree boy into a man who grew more cynical and more easily bored year by year.

It was only when he was with his Regiment that he had shown the enthusiasm which made her happy for him even though she was beset with anxiety that he might fall victim to the might of Napoleon's armies.

It had been an inexpressible relief when on his father's death the Marquis had bought himself out of the Regiment and come home to administer his Estates and to look after her.

At the same time, she knew the boy she had adored for thirty-three years had gone forever.

There had been women in his life, dozens of them. Some she had met, but some lived in a world into which she could never enter.

But her love for him told her they meant nothing to him, and if they suffered a broken heart his was never involved.

Ever since then she had hated the girl who had hurt him.

But she thought now that she hated her even more than before, for it was her fault that Gallen, her beloved son, was making a marriage of convenience rather than one of love.

But the Dowager Marchioness was wise enough to know it was quite useless to say these things aloud.

"When do you plan to be married, my dearest?" she asked.

"Before the end of the Season," the Marquis replied. "The Prince will undoubtedly offer to have the Reception at Carlton House, since the number of people who will expect to be invited could certainly not squeeze into the Earl of Fernleigh's town house in Curzon Street."

"Tell me about the Earl," the Dowager Marchioness said with an effort. "I remember him as being rather a good-looking man, which of course would account for his daughter's beauty."

"He is quite pleasant," the Marquis answered cautiously. "He prefers the country to London, but his wife's life is entirely bound up in Balls, Receptions, Assemblies, and riots."

There was a twist to his lips as he said:

"She was determined that her daughter should be the talk of the town and she has certainly succeeded."

The Dowager Marchioness remembered the Countess of Fernleigh and recalled that she was a woman with whom she had nothing in common.

"I will of course call on the Countess on my return south," she said, "but I thought I would go home and not to London."

Home was a very attractive Dower House in the grounds of the Marquis's huge Estate in Huntingdonshire.

The Marquis knew that his mother, now that she suffered so acutely from arthritis, disliked having to be in London and was much happier in the country with her dogs and her garden.

"There will be no need for you to come to London before the wedding," he said. "I will invite the Earl and of course Beryl to the Castle as soon as you are ready to see them."

He smiled as he added:

"I dare say there will be time before the wedding, although doubtless Beryl will be continuously engaged in buying her trousseau."

"And you, dearest?" his mother enquired.

"The Prince likes me to be in regular attendance on him," the Marquis replied. "I have come to the more or less amicable arrangement that I escort him to races and other amusements in the daytime, but I am relieved of attending most of the overcrowded and certainly overheated parties that His Royal Highness enjoys in the evening."

"What do you do instead?" the Dowager Marchioness asked.

"That is a very indiscreet question, Mama," the Marquis replied, his eyes twinkling.

His mother gave a little laugh.

"I am not asking what you did in the past. I am well aware of your reputation as a lady-killer. But what will you do now? I am sure Lady Beryl will wish you to escort her to what you call the 'overcrowded and overheated' crushes."

"The penalties of an engaged man!" the Marquis said lightly. "But I assure you, Mama, that I find a green baize table more enticing than a polished floor, and I have no intention of staying up until dawn every night whether Beryl or the Prince commands me to do so."

The Dowager Marchioness smiled.

"I know that you have some new horses you are breaking in and wish to ride very early each morning."

"A dozen magnificent thoroughbreds. I am looking forward to showing them to you."

"And I shall be looking forward to seeing them," the Dowager Marchioness replied.

One of the great benefits that peace with France had brought to those who loved fine horseflesh was that horses could now be brought into England again.

The Marquis had sent to Syria for some Arab mares, which had arrived only the previous month.

When he spoke of his horses his mother thought there was a note in his voice that was different from the way in which he spoke of his future bride.

In February, before she had come to Harrogate, several Hungarian horses had been brought to the Castle, and to her delight she had caught an echo of the child who had run eagerly to draw her by the hand down to the stables when he had a new pony.

"Is Lady Beryl a good rider?" she asked now.

"She looks well on a horse," the Marquis answered, "and of course she will hunt with my own pack. That reminds me, I must do up the Hunting Lodge in Leicestershire."

He smiled somewhat mockingly as he added:

"The bachelor parties I have given there have not improved the condition of the furnishings, and I suspect that any woman would find it distressingly masculine."

"Your father and I had some very happy times there," the Dowager Marchioness said wistfully.

"As you had everywhere," the Marquis answered. "And now, Mama, stop comparing me with Papa and yourself with Beryl."

He moved to take her hands once again into his as he said:

"You know without my telling you there will never be another woman as sweet or as beautiful as you! So it is no use complaining if I have to accept second best."

"All I want, dearest, is your happiness," the Dowager Marchioness murmured.

"I have already told you I am content," the Marquis replied.

His mother thought as he spoke that there was a distinctly cynical note in his voice.

* * *

Some miles away from the fashionable Harrogate resort, with its Spa, its expensive Hotels, and its aristocratic visitors, but still in Yorkshire, was the village of Barrowfield.

Near Leeds, it was a village of poorly built, dilapidated, dismal houses which always seemed to be covered with a fine veil of coal-dust.

Outside the village and built on a hill rising above it was an ugly grey stone Church and beside it an equally ugly and unnecessarily large Vicarage.

In the kitchen, with its unwieldy, out-of-date stove and flagged floor, a servant with grey hair and the neat appearance of a children's nurse was trying to instruct a thin, rather vacant-looking girl how to baste a leg of mutton.

"Try to understand what I am saying, Ellen,"

the older woman said sharply. "I've told you six times already to keep spooning the gravy over the meat, but you don't seem to understand me."

"Oi'm doing wha' ya tells me," the girl replied in a broad Yorkshire accent.

"That's a matter of opinion," the older woman snapped.

Then she turned her head as the kitchen door opened and a young voice cried:

"Abby! Abby!"

Abigail, for that was her full name, turned from the stove to look at the girl coming into the kitchen.

With her fair hair and blue eyes, she could have been described as being typically English in appearance, if it had not been for the almost arresting loveliness of her face.

Her eyes seemed almost too big for the oval of it, and although they were blue they were the deep blue of a southern sea rather than a spring sky.

People who looked closely at Torilla noticed the sweetness of her mouth, the lips softly curved and the faint smile that seemed to lift the corners almost like sunshine peeping through the leaves of a tree.

"What is it, Miss Torilla?" Abby enquired.

"A letter, Abby! A letter from Lady Beryl, and—would you believe it?—she is engaged to be married!"

"And about time," Abby said with the familiarity of an old servant. "Her Ladyship must be getting on for twenty-one, and with all her success in London I expected her to be married long before this."

"Well, she is engaged now," Torilla said, "and what do you think, Abby? She begs me to go and stay with her!"

She looked down at the letter and read aloud:

"You must be My Bridesmaid, Torilla. I intend to have only One so as not to pro-

*vide Myself with unnecessary Competi-
tion."*

Torilla laughed.

"As if there could be any competition where
Beryl is concerned!"

Abby did not answer and she went on reading:

*"You must come to Me immediately You get
this Letter. Do not Delay. There are so
many Things with which I wish You to help
Me—My clothes, the planning of My
Marriage, and of course there will be dozens
of Parties at which People will Wish to meet
My Fiancé."*

"And who's Her Ladyship's intended?" Abby
inquired.

Torilla looked again at the letter and turned the
pages.

"You will hardly believe this, Abby," she answered, "but she does not say his name!"

She gave a little laugh.

"Is not that just like Beryl? She always forgets
something important. I can see I shall have my hands
full looking after her, that is if Papa . . . will let me . . .
go."

Her voice dropped on the last words and there
was an expression of doubt in her big eyes.

"Of course you must go, Miss Torilla," Abby
said firmly, "though goodness knows what you will
have to wear."

"We need not worry about that," Torilla replied.
"Beryl's clothes fit me and she was always generous
enough to let me wear anything I required, even her
riding-habits."

There was suddenly a wistful expression on her
face before she said:

"Oh, Abby, do you think I shall be allowed to ride Uncle Hector's horses? It would be so wonderful to be on the back of a fine piece of horseflesh once again."

"I'm sure your uncle will be only too pleased to mount you as he did when you were a child."

"I think horses are what I have missed here more than anything else," Torilla said.

"There's a good many things I've missed," Abby retorted, "and you've missed as well, Miss Torilla, if you're honest."

As she spoke, Abby started to take off the brown holland apron she had put on for cooking over the spotless white one she wore with her grey dress.

"I'm going to start packing for you right this minute," she said.

"No, Abby, wait, wait!" Torilla cried. "I must ask Papa first. He may not wish me to go . . . home."

She said the word tentatively, then added almost apologetically:

"I always think of Fernford as . . . home—as it was for seventeen years until Mama . . . died."

"That's right, Miss Torilla. It *is* home!" Abby said firmly. "It's where you belong. We should never have come to this dirty place, and that's the truth!"

Torilla smiled.

She had heard Abby say this not once but a thousand times.

"You know what it means to Papa," she said softly.

As she spoke she heard the sound of the front door closing.

"There he is!" she exclaimed. "Hurry with the luncheon, Abby, or you know as well as I do he will rush out again without having anything to eat. I will go and talk to him."

Before she finished the last words she turned and sped from the kitchen along the narrow gloomy passage which led into the somewhat pretentious Hall.

Standing just inside the front door was the Reverend Augustus Clifford, Vicar of Barrowfield.

He was a handsome man who looked older than his years.

His hair was almost completely grey, his too-thin face deeply lined, and he had the appearance of a man who drove himself beyond his strength.

As he put his clergyman's hat down on the chair he was looking worried, but as he saw Torilla coming towards him he smiled.

"You see I am back, Torilla!" he said. "And on time, as you told me to be."

"That was good of you, Papa, and luncheon is ready," Torilla answered. "I could not have borne it if you had ruined the very nice leg of mutton which Farmer Shipton gave us."

"Yes, of course, I had not forgotten," the Vicar said, "and if it is large enough perhaps we could share . . ."

"No, Papa!" Torilla said firmly. "There is not enough to share with anyone, but come into the Dining-Room, for I have something to tell you."

The Vicar obeyed her and they walked into the small dark room which unlike the Drawing-Room looked out at the front of the house and therefore faced north.

There were a few pieces of good furniture they had brought with them from the south, but the curtains were of cheap material, although Abby and Torilla had done their best to copy one of the draped pelmets they had seen at Fernleigh Hall.

The Countess of Fernleigh's younger sister Elizabeth had married Augustus Clifford when he was a curate at St. George's Hanover Square, London.

The Earl of Fernleigh to oblige his wife had appointed him Vicar of the small Parish of Fernford on his Estate in Hertfordshire, and Torilla and Beryl had grown up together.

For the first cousins it had been a very happy

arrangement, and although Beryl was two years older than Torilla the difference in their ages had not been obvious.

Torilla was in fact far cleverer than her cousin, and it had not been so much a case of her trying to keep up with the older girl as of Beryl lagging behind her when it came to lessons.

The Countess of Fernleigh preferred to spend most of the year in London and therefore Beryl spent more time with her aunt than she did with her mother.

She had loved Mrs. Clifford, and when she died unexpectedly one cold winter she had been almost as grief-stricken as Torilla.

Losing her mother had completely changed Torilla's whole way of life.

The Reverend Augustus had decided that the only possible thing for him to do was to leave the house where he had been so happy with his wife.

He no longer wished to work in the quiet country village where as a matter of fact there had been little for him to do.

He had applied to be sent to one of the most desolate and poverty-stricken areas in the north, and two months after his wife's death he had been appointed to Barrowfield.

It had all happened so quickly that Torilla could hardly realise what was happening, until she found herself in a strange, alien place away from everything that was familiar, with only Abby to cling to in her unhappiness.

To the Reverend Augustus it was a relief from his misery and also a challenge which no-one had realised he wanted all his life.

Driven by a fervent desire to help those less fortunate than himself, and imbued with a crusading spirit, he flung himself wholeheartedly into the problems and difficulties he found in the terrifying squalor of a mining village.

It was as if he took on the hosts of evil entirely by himself.

Only Torilla and Abby knew that in his fervor he would, if they had not prevented him, have gone without food and sleep in his efforts to improve the conditions he found in his new Parish.

Every penny of his stipend and the little money he had of his own was spent on the people for whom he worked.

It was only because Abby insisted on his giving her enough money for the housekeeping as soon as the cheques came in that they were saved from starvation.

As she seated herself now at the Dining-Room table Torilla knew that the real difficulty in getting her father's permission to go south would be the cost of the journey.

"I have had a letter from Beryl, Papa," she said as the Vicar poured himself a glass of water, and Abby came in through the door carrying the leg of mutton.

"From Beryl?" the Vicar asked vaguely, as if he had never heard the name.

"Beryl is to be married, Papa. She begs me to go and stay at the Hall and help her with her trousseau. And she has asked me to be her bridesmaid."

"Oh, Beryl!" the Vicar exclaimed, picking up the carving-knife and starting to slice the mutton.

"You will not mind if I go, Papa?" Torilla asked.

"No, no. Of course not," the Vicar replied.

Then as he cut a slice and put it on the plate he added:

"But I doubt if we can afford it."

"I will go by Stage-Coach," Torilla said, "and if I go alone and leave Abby to look after you, it will not cost so very much."

She had thought at first when Beryl's letter came that she would be able to take Abby with her, but now she knew, not only because of the expense but because the Vicar would not look after himself, that Abby must stay with him.

Abby could bully him into eating and sleeping more effectively even than Torilla herself could do.

"I was thinking," the Vicar said, almost as if he were talking to himself, "that any spare money we have should go to Mrs. Coxwold. She is expecting her ninth child and I am sure the oldest girl has consumption."

"I am very sorry for the Coxwolds, Papa," Torilla answered, "but you know as well as I do that Mr. Coxwold goes to the Public House every Friday evening and drinks away at least half his wages."

"I know—I know," the Vicar said, "but a man is entitled to spend what he earns."

"Not when his children are starving," Torilla retorted.

"The second girl will be five this month and I think they will send her to work in the mine."

"Oh, no, Papa!" Torilla cried. "She is too young! You remember how ill the little Barnsby child was after she had worked in water up to her knees and contracted pneumonia."

The Vicar sighed.

"They have to eat, Torilla."

"And so have you, Sir," Abby said, coming back into the room.

She carried two dishes, one of which contained potatoes and the other some rather unappetising-looking cabbage.

"I have enough," the Vicar said vaguely, looking at the very small pieces of meat on his plate.

"I'm not taking this mutton off the table 'til you've helped yourself properly, Sir," Abby said in the affectionate bullying tones of a Nanny talking to a recalcitrant child.

The Vicar picked up the carvers and added two small slices to those on his plate.

Having stood with the vegetables at the Vicar's side until he had helped himself to two tablespoonfuls of potatoes, Abby waited in the room until Torilla had finished before she said:

"I wonder, Miss Torilla, if you would get the suet pudding out of the oven for me. I don't trust that girl. The treacle is here so all we need now is the pudding."

"Yes, of course," Torilla said obediently.

Abby handed her the mutton and she carried it out to the kitchen, knowing as she went that Abby would speak to her father.

"Miss Torilla has told you, Sir," Abby said as soon as she had left the room, "that Her Ladyship has asked her to go south for her wedding."

"Yes, Miss Torilla has told me," the Vicar replied. "The fact is, Abby, we cannot afford it. Stage-Coaches cost money and it is a long way to Hertford-shire."

"But it's high time, Sir, if you'll excuse me for speaking frankly, that Miss Torilla went back and saw some decent folk for a change."

The Vicar looked up in surprise and Abby went on before he could speak:

"Do you realise that Miss Torilla's been here nearly two years and hasn't exchanged half-a-dozen words with a Lady or a Gentleman? Her poor mother would turn in her grave if she knew what sort of place you've brought her to, and that's the truth!"

The Vicar looked startled.

"I have not thought of that, Abby."

"Well, I have, Sir! Miss Torilla's eighteen, and if Mrs. Clifford were alive, God rest her soul, she would be looking out for a suitable husband for Miss Torilla, giving parties for her, and having friends of her own age to the house."

Abby snorted before she went on:

"What sort of people could we invite here? Ragged, dirty creatures covered in coal-dust."

She spoke scathingly, but as the Vicar put up his hand she added:

"Oh, I know, Sir, they've souls to save, they're Christians, and they're the same as us in the sight of God. But you're not expecting Miss Torilla to marry a coal-miner, are you, Sir?"

The Vicar looked uncomfortable.

"To tell you the truth, Abby, I had not thought of Miss Torilla as being grown up."

"Well, she is, Sir, and it's a crying shame—it is really—that she should be buried alive—because that's what it is—in this dreadful place."

"I am needed here," the Vicar said in a low voice, almost as if he was pleading his case in the Dock.

"That's as may be," Abby replied, "and I'm not saying, Sir, that you're not doing the work of God, and doing it well. It's your chosen profession, so to speak. But Miss Torilla's not a Parson nor a Preacher, she's a young woman, and very beautiful one at that!"

There was no time to say more because Torilla came back into the room with a small suet pudding in the centre of a rather large dish.

She set it down in front of her father and for a moment he did not seem to see it, as, deep in his thoughts, he appeared to be quite oblivious of her presence.

Torilla looked rather anxiously at Abby. Then as the maid changed the plates and placed a tablespoon in the Vicar's hand he said:

"You are right, Abby. Miss Torilla must go to Lady Beryl's wedding. We will find the money somehow."

It was after he had rushed out of the house, almost before he had finished the last mouthful of the suet pudding, that Torilla said to Abby:

"You made Papa agree! Oh, Abby, I feel so guilty. You could see he was upset at having to spend so much on me. He wanted the money for the Coxwolds."

"Those Coxwolds have had more than their

share of your father's money already," Abby said crossly. "That woman's a whiner, and the Vicar, poor man, believes every word she tells him."

"Yes, I know, Abby, but he does suffer so greatly and this place is terrible. I cannot bear to look at the children."

There was a little sob in Torilla's voice as she added:

"Perhaps it is ... selfish of me. If I stay and Papa gives the money to the Coxwolds it might make all the ... difference to them."

"If there are a hundred Coxwolds dying on their feet," Abby said firmly, "they'll not stop you from going to stay with Lady Beryl."

"Perhaps it is wrong of me to leave Papa," Torilla murmured.

"If you refuse the invitation it'll be over my dead body!" Abby said. "Now sit down, Miss Torilla, and write and tell Her Ladyship you'll leave here next Monday."

"But, Abby, that is the day after tomorrow!"

"The sooner the better," Abby snapped, "and you needn't worry about your father either. I'll look after him, you know that."

"He pays far more attention to you than to me," Torilla said. "I could never have persuaded him to eat those extra pieces of mutton, and I think he enjoyed them, although he did not say so."

"That leg of mutton's going to last us 'til the end of the week," Abby said. "What your father needs is more good square meals inside him, then he'd not worry so acutely over the poor and the sick."

Torilla knew that was true; at the same time, her father was not the only one who suffered.

She could not bear to see the small children who worked in the mine and were whipped if they cried or fell asleep. She felt sick when she saw women who by the age of thirty were old and infirm cripples.

She could understand why the men in this dirty,

soul-destroying existence hurried to the Public House every Friday night to forget for an hour or so the dangers of their work in the darkness of the pit.

Whenever there was an accident her father would come home white-faced and almost in tears, and she would take the broth that Abby made to the women who were ill and to the children who never had enough to eat.

But they had little enough to spare.

If Abby had not bullied her father from time to time into giving her a few shillings to buy some cheap material, Torilla knew that she would have gone as threadbare as some of the wives of the miners.

There were pitifully few gowns to pack but Abby spent the next day washing and ironing, pressing and sewing.

Torilla had also a few clothes left which had belonged to her mother, pretty frocks and evening-gowns which she had had no opportunity to wear in the grime and isolation of Barrowfield.

She was afraid that they were out-of-date. But she had no way of gauging whether or not this was true; for they had no money to waste on the *Ladies Journal* or any magazine which showed sketches of what was being worn in London.

Torilla, however, was not worried about her appearance, since she knew that Beryl would be as generous to her as she had always been.

Wearing a cloak which was somewhat threadbare over a plain muslin gown, and a chip-straw bonnet trimmed with cheap blue ribbons, she left the Vicarage early on Monday morning to catch the Stage-Coach which was to carry her on the first part of her journey.

"You oughtn't to be travelling alone, and that's a fact!" Abby said as they waited at the cross-roads for the Coach which started from Leeds.

"Well, we can hardly pretend I am a babe in arms," Torilla answered with a smile, "and there is no other way by which I could travel on one ticket."

"Now don't you go talking to strangers," Abby admonished, "and that reminds me—there's something I want to say to you, Miss Torilla."

"What is that?" Torilla asked a little apprehensively.

"For the last two years, dearie, you've lived a strange, unnatural life for a young girl, with nothing but misery, poverty, and squalor round you. What I want to say is—don't you go talking about it too much when you're with Her Ladyship."

"Why not?" Torilla asked.

"Because people don't want to listen to such things, Miss Torilla. They want to talk about happy things, not miserable ones."

Abby paused a moment before she went on:

"Do you remember how your mother used to say to the Master: 'Cheer up, darling, you can't take all the worries and sins of the world on your shoulders'?"

Torilla gave a little smile.

"Yes, I remember Mama saying that, and Papa used to ask: 'Am I being a bore?'"

"That's right," Abby said, "and since your dear mother passed away that's exactly what the Master has become, Miss Torilla, to other people."

"I don't think him a bore!" Torilla exclaimed loyally.

"No, dear, but other people would," Abby said, "and that's why when you're away from here forget what you've seen and what you've heard, and just go back into the sunshine of life as it was when you were at home."

She said the last words deliberately and she saw the sudden light in Torilla's blue eyes.

She knew she was thinking of how happy they had all been in the Vicarage that stood in a clean attractive village of thatched cottages with flower-filled gardens.

"You promise me," Abby said insistently.

"That I will not be a bore?" Torilla asked. "Yes,

of course I promise, but oh, Abby, I wish you were coming with me! If anyone deserves a holiday it is you!"

"It'll be a holiday for me thinking of you having a bit of fun for a change," Abby replied.

She looked up the road and saw the Stage-Coach in the distance.

"Here it comes!" she exclaimed. "Now have a lovely time, dearie. Enjoy every moment of it and just forget everything else."

"I will never forget you, dear Abby," Torilla said.

She put her arms round the old maid's neck and kissed her on both cheeks.

"Thank you for promising to look after Papa. It is all thanks to you that I can be at Beryl's wedding."

"Tell Her Ladyship I'll be wishing her every happiness," Abby said, "and I hope she's got a man who's worthy of her."

"I hope so, too," Torilla answered.

The Stage-Coach, its roof heavily laden with luggage and a number of male passengers sitting on top, rumbled to a standstill beside them.

The guard jumped down to pick up Torilla's small round-topped trunk and place it on the roof, before opening the Coach door.

Torilla saw that there was one place left between two large, fat people taking up more than their fair share of the back seat.

"Good-bye, Abby," she said and climbed in, apologising for knocking against the passengers' feet as she did so.

She sat down, the guard climbed up on the box, and Torilla bent forward to wave her hand.

Abby waved back. She was smiling, although there were tears in her eyes, as the coachman whipped up the horses and the Stage-Coach started off again.

Chapter Two

The Marquis of Havingham drove his team of four perfectly matched chestnuts with a flourish into the court-yard of the Peligan Inn.

He was driving in his specially built travelling Phaeton, which was lighter and therefore faster than any other vehicle on the road.

"I think we have done a record today, Jim," the Marquis remarked.

"A fine performance, M'Lord," Jim replied, knowing he would be able to relate it with relish to the other grooms whom he would meet in the Tap-Room.

The Marquis looked round the crowded yard with dismay.

There were far more fashionable vehicles resting on their shafts than he had expected and after a moment he exclaimed:

"Of course! Doncaster Races. I had forgotten them!"

"I expect Your Lordship'll be comfortable enough," Jim said soothingly. "Mr. Harris'll have seen to that."

The Marquis had no doubts on that score, for by sending his valet ahead with his luggage he was always assured that the most comfortable rooms would be provided for him and that on his arrival everything he required would be waiting and ready.

He was however well aware that a race-meeting in any town brought in the Quality from far and near.

It meant that the Inn staff would be run off their feet and it would inevitably be noisy, which after a long day on the road was something he disliked extremely.

But nothing could be done about it now, and as he stepped down from his Phaeton he almost regretted that he had not arranged to stay with friends as he had done on his way north.

"Who will you visit when you leave here?" his mother had asked before he left.

"I have decided to go south as quickly as possible," the Marquis replied, "and quite frankly, Mama, I found that the majority of people with whom I stayed on my way here were excessively boring."

He did not add that one of the reasons for this was that he had found that the owners of the large and comfortable mansions who had welcomed him effusively had a habit of trying to thrust one of their daughters upon him.

He had enjoyed the few days he had spent at Woburn Abbey at Burleigh, and with the Duke of Darlington at his extremely impressive country house.

But the manoeuvres of his hostesses to engage his interest in their usually plain, tongue-tied daughters had made the Marquis long for the sophisticated, witty, and beguiling women with whom he spent his time in London.

They were fortunately all married and, what was more, knew the rules of the game; so there was no chance of his being threatened with a wedding-ring, which in his private view was as inhibiting as a pair of hand-cuffs.

As he was already betrothed to Beryl Fern, the machinations with regard to matrimony which he had encountered only too often over the years had on this occasion irritated him all the more.

He had decided when he reached Harrogate that he had no intention of subjecting himself once again to the boredom of it.

"But you hate Inns and Hotels, dearest," his mother had remarked in surprise.

"I know, Mama, but I only have to endure them for one night at a time, and Harris makes me as comfortable as it is humanly possible to be in such circumstances."

"I would be happier if you stayed with friends," the Dowager Marchioness insisted.

"But I would not!" the Marquis replied. "So cease worrying, Mama, and as usual I shall travel incognito."

The Marquis was not only of paramount Social importance but he was known as a race-horse owner over the length and breadth of the country.

This made him decide, when he stayed in Inns or Posting Houses, to use one of his minor titles.

He knew now that Harris would have booked him in at The Peligan as Sir Alexander Abdy.

He would not therefore be disturbed by the "hangers-on" who always surrounded him on race-courses or who besieged him in London with pleas for help or, more difficult, pretensions to friendships forged during the war.

He walked in through the side-door of The Peligan which opened onto the court-yard and found, as he had expected, that Harris was waiting.

Beside him was his senior groom, whom he had also sent ahead in charge of his horses.

"Good-evening, M'Lord," both men said simultaneously.

"An excellent run, Ben," the Marquis said to the groom. "Those new chestnuts are worth every penny I paid for them."

"I'm glad to hear that, M'Lord."

"I pushed them hard today," the Marquis said, "so you will have to take them easily tomorrow. Watch that new groom, he is a thruster."

"I will, M'Lord."

The Marquis followed Harris along a narrow passage and up an ancient oak staircase.

As he went he could hear the noise in the Coffee-Room and knew that the race-goers were already celebrating or drowning their sorrows after a day on the course.

As Harris showed him into a pleasant bed-room with a bow-window and a four-poster bed which looked as if it might be passably comfortable, the Marquis said:

"I had forgotten that the races were taking place at Doncaster this week."

"I thinks Your Lordship might have done that," Harris replied, "but as we never enters our animals for the Spring Meeting, I'm afraid, M'Lord, it also slipped my memory."

The Marquis was used to his senior servants identifying themselves with him and his possessions and he merely said:

"I suppose the place is damned crowded, as might be expected."

"I regret to say it is, M'Lord, but a private room's been engaged and I doubt if Your Lordship'll be very inconvenienced."

He paused before he added tentatively:

"I'm sorry, however, to tell you, M'Lord, that I was unable to engage also the bed-room next to this."

The Marquis said nothing and Harris helping him off with his coat continued:

"It's only a slip of a room, M'Lord, and I persuaded the Inn-keeper not to let it to one of the gentlemen who I thought might be noisy, but to a lady who'd not be likely to disturb Your Lordship."

Again the Marquis did not reply, but it irritated

him to think that if anyone was banging about next door he would be unable to sleep.

Owing, he supposed, to a very active brain, he liked complete quiet when he retired to bed, and he made every effort to secure it.

It was therefore on his explicit instructions that his servants always engaged the adjoining bed-room to his own, and if necessary one on either side.

He was well aware it was his own fault that on this occasion such an arrangement had not been possible; in fact he told himself philosophically that he was lucky to obtain accommodation at all during race-week.

He was quite certain, although he did not ask, that Harris had over-bid some unfortunate who employed less-generous-handed servants.

He would have also tipped the staff so handsomely that whoever else was neglected or overlooked in The Peligan it would not be he.

The Marquis had a bath in front of the fire, and afterwards, dressed in his evening-clothes, he went downstairs to a small but comfortable private Sitting-Room.

There was a fire to keep him warm, the dinner was excellent, and, as he had expected, the service was impeccable.

When the meal was finished he sat by the fireside to sip a glass of brandy and peruse the newspapers with which Harris had provided him.

He noted with satisfaction that the horses running in the races were not up to his standard and would not have afforded his stable a challenge.

If there was one thing the Marquis disliked where his horses were concerned it was a "walk-over."

He told himself that he had been right in competing at Doncaster only in the St. Leger, which was run in September.

He was in fact concentrating on Ascot this year because he was determined to win the Gold Cup.

He glanced at the other news in the paper and found the usual complaints about the difficulties the country was experiencing in adjusting itself to peace. The Parliamentary reports were dry and dull as usual.

The warmth of the fire, after he had been in the air all day, made him feel sleepy and finishing his brandy he went upstairs far earlier than was usual, to find Harris waiting to help him undress.

When he slept in public Inns or Hotels his valet always brought not only the Marquis's own linen sheets with which to make the bed but his down pillows.

"Would Your Lordship wish to be called early?" Harris asked.

He had the Marquis's clothes over his arm, ready to be packed.

The following morning he would leave the Pelican as soon as it was light, to travel ahead as he had done today, so as to have everything in readiness for his Master's arrival.

"Eight o'clock will be soon enough," the Marquis answered. "You have left my clothes ready for Jim?"

"They're all in the wardrobe, M'Lord," Harris replied.

There was a touch of reproach in his voice that the Marquis should find it necessary to query his arrangements.

It had been an excellent idea, the Marquis thought, that Jim, who was his groom, should also, when required, be able to valet him.

"Good-night, M'Lord." Harris said respectfully. "I hopes Your Lordship is not disturbed."

"I hope so too," the Marquis replied.

Harris took a last glance round to see that everything was in order, then went from the room, closing the door behind him.

The Marquis took off his long silk robe, threw it on a chair, and got into bed.

He was right in thinking that the bed looked comfortable, the mattress being made of goose-feathers.

As he sank into it he thought with satisfaction that the evening spent alone had really been far preferable to having to listen to the conversation of a boring host.

Worse still, because of his importance he usually found on his arrival at some country mansion that a dinner-party had been arranged in his honour.

This meant he was expected to make himself pleasant to a number of people with whom he had nothing in common, had never seen before, and in most cases hoped never to see again.

His linen sheets were fine and cool, and there was only the fire-light to dispense a golden glow on the shadows in the room.

The Marquis was in fact almost asleep when he heard heavy, somewhat uncertain footsteps coming up the oak stairs.

Vaguely at the back of his mind he wondered why the devil the Inn-keepers could not have carpet fitted on their stairs like other civilised folk.

Then, so loud that it made him start, there was a knock on the door.

For a moment he thought it was on his own. Then as the knock was repeated, he realised that it was in fact on the door of the next room.

"Who is . . . it?"

It was a woman's voice that asked the question and her voice was low.

Yet the Marquis could hear her quite clearly, and he thought angrily that the communicating wall between their rooms was too thin.

"Oi've sommat to give ye that ye left in th' Dining-Room, Miss," a man's voice replied.

He spoke in a strange accent which the Marquis could not place, but merely thought it sounded unusual.

"But I am . . . sure I left nothing . . . behind!" the woman protested.

"Oi've got it 'ere, Miss."

The Marquis tried not to think of what was going

on, but he imagined that the woman, whoever she was, was getting out of bed.

Then he heard the sound of the key turning in the lock.

"I cannot imagine . . ." she said, then her voice ceased before she exclaimed: "Oh . . . it is . . . you!"

"Yes, it is I," the man said in an entirely different accent. "You slipped away without saying good-night."

"I had . . . nothing to say . . . and you had no right, Sir, to . . . speak to me. . . ."

"But I want to speak to you."

"You should not have . . . come here. . . . Please go . . . away."

The Marquis had the idea that the woman was trying to shut the door. Then she gave a cry:

"No! No! You are not to come in! Go away . . . go away at . . . once!"

"I want to talk to you."

"P-please . . . leave me alone . . . you cannot come into my . . . bed-room."

"I am in! What do you intend to do about it?"

"You have no right . . . I shall scream for help if you do not . . . leave at . . . once!"

"I doubt if the Inn-keeper or anyone else will hear you. They are busy downstairs."

"Will you please . . . go! I have . . . gone to bed . . . and I have . . . nothing to say to . . . you."

"But I have a great deal to say to you! You are very lovely, Miss Clifford. You see, I have learnt your name, even though you would not give it to me."

"Y-you must . . . leave . . . it is wrong . . . you know it is wrong . . . to force your way into m-my . . . bed-room like this!"

"I see nothing wrong about it, and if you will stop putting on these airs and graces we can enjoy ourselves."

"I do not . . . know what you mean. . . . Please go . . . please, please leave me . . . alone!"

"That, my dear, is something I have no intention

of doing. Now come along—be sensible. You attract me. I have not seen anyone so lovely for a long time."

The man must have moved, and now there was a scream that was unmistakably one of fear.

"No . . . no!"

Quite suddenly the Marquis sat up in bed.

It was intolerable, he thought, that not only should he be disturbed but that any woman should be insulted in this disgraceful manner.

He realised from the conversation after the man had entered her room that he was in fact a gentleman. The way he had spoken to bring her to the door had been the assumed voice of how he thought a servant would speak.

Now his tones were cultured, although at the same time slurred, which told the Marquis that he had been drinking.

The Marquis was no prude and if he desired a woman he pursued her. But he would not have considered it sporting to foist his attentions on any woman who was clearly unwilling.

Certainly he would not have approached one who was travelling alone and was therefore unprotected and extremely vulnerable.

There was another scream and now the Marquis jumped out of bed and pulling on his robe opened his own door and went into the passage.

The door of the room next door was shut and he opened it without knocking.

As he entered he saw as he had expected a woman struggling desperately in the arms of a man.

The Marquis recognised him immediately as a habitual race-goer. Known as Sir Joscelyn Threnton, he was to be found at the bar of any race-course and his associates were those whom the Marquis suspected of evading where possible the rules of the Jockey Club.

Sir Joscelyn was so intent on trying to kiss the woman in his arms that he did not see the Marquis enter.

Torilla therefore saw him first.

"Help me! Help me!" she cried.

In two strides the Marquis crossed the small room and taking Sir Joscelyn by the shoulder pulled him round to face him.

"Get out of here!" he said sharply.

Sir Joscelyn started to say furiously:

"What the hell's it got to do with . . . ?"

Then as he realised to whom he was speaking, his voice died away into silence.

"Get out!"

There was no need for the Marquis to say any more.

Sir Joscelyn opened his lips as if either to explain his behaviour or query the Marquis's authority to give him orders, but then he thought better of it.

With a look of defiance on his face but at once and without dignity he slouched out of the room and there was the sound of his footsteps clattering down the oak stairs.

The Marquis looked at the woman he had rescued and realised she was very young and very lovely.

Her fair hair fell almost to her waist, and her eyes, wide and terror-stricken, seemed to fill the whole of her small face.

She was standing only a few inches from the wall of the small room and now she moved forward a step to say in a low, frightened little voice:

"Thank you . . . thank you for . . . saving me . . . I did not . . . know what . . . to do."

"It is intolerable that you should have been subjected to anything so unpleasant," the Marquis said. "He will not return, but lock your door and do not open it again."

"I . . . it was very . . . foolish of me to have done so . . . but I never thought . . . I never dreamt . . . there were . . . men like that in the . . . world."

The Marquis could not help smiling.

"Now you know there are, so be more careful in the future."

"I . . . will," she answered, "and . . . thank you again . . . I am . . . very grateful."

"Go to sleep and forget about it," the Marquis said as if he were speaking to a child.

He went out, closing the door behind him, and before he reached his own room he heard the key turn in the lock.

As he got into bed he thought he could understand Sir Joscelyn taking a fancy to the very pretty girl who was sleeping next door.

He had said it was a long time since he had seen anyone so lovely and the Marquis thought he spoke the truth.

He wondered who she was and why she was travelling alone. Then he remembered that Sir Joscelyn had called her "Miss Clifford."

'It is not an unusual name,' the Marquis thought, 'but she is obviously a lady. Her hair is the colour of spring sunshine.'

Then he laughed at himself for being poetic and fell asleep.

* * *

It was a long time before Torilla's frightened heart-beats began to subside and when she got back into bed she lay trembling.

Never had she expected that a gentleman would dare to force his way into her bed-room.

She had seen him looking at her in the Coffee-Room while he sat there with a number of other gentlemen.

They had grown noisier and more uproarious as the dinner progressed, and Torilla realised they were drinking too freely.

At the table in the far corner where she sat with the other passengers from the Stage-Coach, a few of the men drank ale but the ladies primly asked for glasses of water.

Since the coach-party was served last, the food was getting cold and they were not given a choice of the more luxurious dishes that were served to the other diners.

Torilla had been too tired to be hungry, but felt impatient at the long time that elapsed between each course since the servants were not interested in their requirements.

She was thinking it was hopeless to wait for dessert when a man's voice asked:

"May I introduce myself?"

She had looked up to see standing beside her the gentleman who had been staring at her in an embarrassing manner all through dinner.

"I am Sir Joscelyn Threnton," he went on, with an air which told Torilla he expected her to be impressed. "Will you join me in a glass of wine?"

"No . . . thank you, Sir," Torilla replied.

"I never take no for an answer," Sir Joscelyn retorted. "Now come along and let us get to know each other."

"I can only . . . repeat . . . no, thank you," Torilla answered.

Sir Joscelyn was just about to argue further when one of his friends called him from the other side of the room.

He turned away from Torilla and with a swiftness born of fear, she slipped from her chair and out of the room without Sir Joscelyn being aware of it.

With her bed-room locked, she had thought she was safe from him.

She had been in bed for some time when she had heard the occupant of the next room speaking to someone she thought must be his valet.

He must have attended the races, she told herself, otherwise it would be unlikely that anyone of any great distinction should stay in a country Inn.

When she had travelled north with her father two years before, the Inns had been almost deserted.

What visitors there were were commercial travellers, professional men, or farmers, and they were not particularly interesting either to look at or to talk to.

Torilla could not help staring wide-eyed at the elegance of some of the gentlemen who had come from the race-course.

It was a long time since she had seen intricately tied muslin cravats, champagne-coloured pantaloons which clung as if their wearers had been poured into them, and Hessian boots polished until they reflected like mirrors.

Her father in his black clerical garments and the miners in their dirty rags were all she had had to look at for two years.

She had never imagined that a man with any pretensions of being a gentleman would behave as Sir Joscelyn had done.

* * *

The Stage-Coach travellers were called at five-thirty A.M. and a maid knocked perfunctorily on Torilla's door to say:

"Yer breakfast's a-waiting, Miss."

Torilla had in fact been awake for some time.

She had dozed a little in the early hours of the morning but kept waking with a start, imagining that Sir Joscelyn was putting out his arms to catch hold of her and she could not escape.

"The sooner I am away from here the better!" she told herself.

She dressed and put her nightgown into the small valise which contained the other things she needed for the night.

She knew it was very unlikely that any of the race-goers would be up so early.

Nevertheless, while she ate the rather unpalatable breakfast which had been provided for her and her fellow travellers, she kept watching the door of the Coffee-Room in case Sir Joscelyn should come in.

Only when the Stage-Coach rolled away from the

Peligan did Torilla heave a sigh of relief and tell herself that she had learnt a lesson she would never forget.

* * *

The Marquis, having breakfasted from a plentiful selection of well-cooked dishes in his private room, left the Hotel at nine-thirty, with a new team of horses, fresh and fidgeting because, like their owner, they wished to be on the road.

It was a clear, sunny day. The air had had a bite in it, but as the sun came out there was a warmth which told the Marquis summer was not far away.

When he was dressed and Jim was just putting his night-things into an expensive leather hold-all, the Marquis had gone onto the landing and looked at the next room.

The door was open and he saw that it was empty.

Vaguely at the back of his mind he remembered while he was still half-asleep hearing soft sounds very early in the morning.

They had in fact been so soft that they had not awakened him completely, and he told himself now that the girl he had rescued the previous evening must have been a Stage-Coach traveller.

The Stage-Coaches left at six o'clock, but the rest of the visitors at the Peligan, the Marquis was sure, would be spending another day at the races.

He had no wish to meet Sir Joscelyn again, so he did not linger in the yard, which was even busier than it had been when he arrived.

Horses were being brought from the stables to be put between the shafts of Phaetons, Chaises, Barouches, and gigs.

The ostlers and private grooms were shouting at each other and the Inn-keeper was running backwards and forwards with bills that must have taken half the night to tot-up.

The Marquis tipped generously, then drove off, anxious to be on the road before there was much traffic, as he had quite a considerable distance to travel before his next port of call.

The whole day went well. The luncheon which he enjoyed at another Posting Inn, having been arranged by Harris, was not only to his satisfaction but he also found the landlord had some excellent claret.

The Marquis bought several dozen bottles and ordered them to be sent south, to add to the enormous amount of wine he had already in his cellars.

He thought it so good that he decided he would ask the Prince, who fancied himself a connoisseur, to taste it.

As he journeyed on he planned a small but amusing dinner-party at which they could sample a variety of different wines which of course would include champagne, the Prince's favourite beverage.

It was only when he had chosen the guests and even the menu that he wondered if his future wife, Beryl, would expect to be present on such an occasion.

He thought it a bore to have women at a dinner where the wine and food were the first objects of interest.

And he told himself that the sooner Beryl understood that if he wished to have a bachelor-party she must make other arrangement for herself, the better.

As he thought of his intended he realised how disappointed his mother had been in his choice of a wife.

He had known that was inevitable as he drove north to break the news of his impending marriage, but he found himself remembering the sadness in the Dowager Marchioness's eyes and the wistful note in her voice.

"She will be happy enough once I am married," he told himself optimistically, "and when we have children she will both love and spoil them."

It occurred to him for the first time that the life Beryl had lived up to now was hardly conducive to contented motherhood.

She was, as he had described her, the life and soul of every party.

She was also always surrounded by a crowd of admiring swains who laughed at everything she said and extolled her as being more witty than she in fact was.

As if he wished to reassure himself, the Marquis thought:

'We like the same sort of things, we lead the same sort of life.'

That, he was sure, was the right foundation on which to build a commendable marriage.

It was growing late in the afternoon but there was still a little way to go before he reached the George and Dragon, where he intended to stay.

As he drove his horses round the corner of a narrow hedge-bordered road he saw a commotion ahead.

The Marquis, who was travelling fast, pulled in his team.

"An accident!" he remarked briefly.

"To th' Stage-Coach, M'Lord," Jim replied.

They drew nearer. The Stage-Coach which was lying at a drunken angle on the left-hand side of the road had obviously just come into collision with a Chaise drawn by two horses which were plunging about, out of control.

The Stage-Coach had been prevented by the hedgerow from turning over completely and the luggage piled on top had fallen into the road. A number of white chickens which had been contained in a coop were fluttering about, squawking loudly.

Their cries were augmented by a bleat of a sheep sewn into a sack which was lying upside down on the grass verge.

There were feminine screams and masculine oaths, while the owner of the Chaise, a middle-aged and furious gentleman, was hurling abuse at the driver of the Stage-Coach.

The latter, ably supported by the guard, was shouting back at him.

The Marquis looked at the turmoil with amusement. Then as it was impossible to pass and it seemed unlikely that anyone intended to clear up the mess, he handed his reins to his groom.

Without haste he stepped down onto the road and walked up to the combatants, his voice clear and authoritative, cutting across their furious interchange.

"Go to the heads of your horses, you fools!"

Both the gentleman who owned the Chaise and the coachman turned to stare at him in astonishment.

"Your horses!" the Marquis said again, and surprisingly they obeyed him.

He then turned to the men who had been scrambling down from the roof of the Coach and pointed to those who had their heads out the windows, being unable to alight owing to the angle at which it lay.

"Get everyone out!" the Marquis ordered. "Then you can right this vehicle, unless you intend to stay here for the rest of the night."

There was a sharpness in his tone which galvanised the men into activity.

A fat farmer's wife was helped out first, crying as she did so:

"Me chickens . . . me poor little chickens . . . they be all crushed!"

She insisted on her rescuers taking a basket from her first, in which remained a few of the day-old chicks she was doubtless taking to market.

As she reached the ground she declared stridently:

"'Tis a disgrace th' way these coachmen drive! Sommat should be done about it—that it should!"

"I agree with you, Ma'am," the Marquis said.

Then as the woman went on worrying about her chickens he turned his attention to an elderly gentleman who, quivering with anger as he was assisted from the Coach, was swearing that every bone in his body was broken.

He was followed by three more men, then last of all the Marquis saw a little oval face with two large, frightened eyes framed by a somewhat battered bonnet.

Torilla stepped out so lightly that she hardly touched the hands of the two men who were only too anxious to help her.

Then as she reached the road she looked up and saw the Marquis.

Her eyes widened and the colour rose in her pale cheeks as he swept his high-crowned hat from his head, saying:

"We meet again, Miss Clifford!"

It seemed as if she had no words with which to answer him, and after looking at her beneath lazy eyelids he returned to the task of sorting out the accident.

The horses that pulled the Chaise were now under control and in a somewhat peremptory manner the Marquis told the middle-aged owner of them to be on his way.

"I intend to sue the company for the damage that has been done to my vehicle," the gentleman said angrily.

"I doubt if you will receive any compensation," the Marquis replied. "But you can always try."

"The driver is drunk—that is perfectly obvious," the gentleman averred.

"They invariably are," the Marquis answered, and walked away, obviously bored with the subject.

Now that one side of the road was clear the Marquis could proceed on his way. But first he set the men who had been on the Coach to work pushing and pulling the unwieldy vehicle back onto the highway.

"Drive more carefully in the future," the Marquis ordered the coachman.

The man was crimson in the face and there

was some truth in the accusation that, even if he was not drunk, he had certainly imbibed more freely than was wise.

To mitigate the severity of his words, the Marquis gave the driver a guinea and he was instantly all smiles and pleasantries.

The Coach was righted, most of the chickens had been collected and returned to their coop, the sheep still bleating plaintively was placed the right way up on the roof, and the passengers began to take their places.

The Marquis walked to where Torilla was standing a little apart from the others.

"Do you know where you are staying tonight?" he asked.

"At an Inn called the George and Dragon," she replied.

"Then I will take you there, for it is where I am bound myself," the Marquis said.

She looked away from him towards the Coach, then back again.

"I . . . would like that . . . but . . ."

"There are no 'buts,'" the Marquis interrupted. "My groom is a very effective chaperon and you will be there quicker and far more comfortably than if you wait for old grumble-boots!"

She smiled, and would have bent down to pick up her valise which she had beside her on the grass verge.

"Leave it," the Marquis ordered.

He helped her into the Phaeton and went round the other side where Jim jumped down to hand him the reins.

The groom picked up the valise and climbed on the seat behind the hood and then they were off, driving smoothly with a speed which soon left the scene of the accident behind.

The Marquis did not speak and after they had driven a little way Torilla glanced at him from under her eye-lashes. He was not only very impressive, she thought, but very handsome. At the same time, he was rather frightening.

Perhaps it was the proud manner in which he held his head and the expression on his face, which was almost disdainful, as if everything and everybody was beneath him.

His features were classical but there were lines running from his nose to the sides of his mouth which she thought were the marks of cynicism, or was it boredom?

She felt suddenly very young and very inexperienced, and she almost wished she were travelling in the Coach rather than with a stranger.

Then he turned to smile at her and quite unreasonably she felt the sun had come out.

"Are you all right?" he asked.

"Your horses are magnificent, Sir!" she replied.

"I am glad you should think so."

"They are finer than any I have ever seen, except perhaps for those you drove yesterday."

The Marquis looked at her in surprise, and she explained:

"I love horses. While we were waiting this morning for the Coach I looked into the stables at the Inn and a groom told me that four superb chestnuts belonged to . . . Sir Alexander Abdy."

She paused before she asked:

"That is you, is it not, Sir?"

"That is my name," the Marquis agreed.

"Then I would . . . like to . . . thank you . . . again," she said in a low voice.

"Forget it," the Marquis said briefly. "There is no need to talk or even to think of anything that is no longer of any consequence. I would like, however, to know who you are."

"I am Torilla Clifford," she answered.

"Torilla," the Marquis repeated. "I do not think I have ever heard that name before. It becomes you."

He saw that even at such a very mild compliment the colour rose in her face, and he told himself he must be careful not to frighten her as she had been frightened already.

He was not used to the company of young girls but he sensed that Torilla was rather exceptional and not only in her looks.

He had not been mistaken when he had thought last night that not only was she very lovely but there was something sensitive about her.

It was an attribute he had found singularly lacking among the daughters of the aristocracy who had been pressed upon him on his journey north.

He talked about his horses, where he had bought them and their breeding. He realised that Torilla, unlike most women, was not pretending but was in fact vitally interested in everything he said.

She also asked him some intelligent questions which told him that she not only loved horses but had studied racing form. He began to wonder who she was and where she came from.

He was not to know that the Earl of Fernleigh had a racing-stable and that Beryl and Torilla as children vied with the stable-boys in picking the winners of every important race.

It was not long before the George and Dragon, an ancient Posting House with a history of highwaymen, came in sight.

"As we are both staying here," the Marquis said, "I should be honoured, Miss Clifford, if you would dine with me this evening."

She looked at him with what he knew was surprise, and he added:

"I have a private room and I am quite certain that the dinner provided for me will be very much better than the menu selected for the Stage-Coach passengers."

"That would not be difficult, judging by last night's meal," Torilla said with a smile.

"Then you will dine with me?"

She looked at him and there was a worried look in her blue eyes.

"It would not be . . . wrong?"

"Wrong?" he questioned.

"I . . . I am travelling . . . alone," she said, "and I do not know . . . if it would be correct for me to . . . accept the invitation of someone to whom I have not been . . . introduced."

She spoke hesitantly and gave him a glance as if she was afraid he might laugh at her.

But the Marquis replied quite gravely:

"I think, considering the unusual circumstances in which we met, we may consider ourselves introduced, Miss Clifford. Moreover, if you are with me there will be no chance of your being subjected to the odious attentions of anyone who might be dining in the Coffee-Room."

He saw a little shiver go through her as she recalled what had happened last night, and she said quickly:

"I would much . . . rather be with . . . you."

"Then that is settled!" the Marquis said. "I am afraid I keep late hours and so I shall not dine until half after seven. But that will give you time to rest."

"Thank you. Thank you . . . very much!" Torilla said in a breathless little voice.

They drove into the court-yard of the George and Dragon and as the landlord hurried forward the Marquis explained Torilla's presence.

"There has been an accident to the Stage-Coach about five miles away from here," he said. "I have brought Miss Clifford, who is one of the passengers, with me. Kindly see she has a comfortable room to herself."

"Just as you say, Sir," the Inn-keeper replied, bowing obsequiously not only to the Marquis but also to Torilla.

She was taken upstairs and given, she was quite

sure, a far more comfortable room than was usually accorded to Stage-Coach passengers.

"He is very kind," she told herself as, doing what the Marquis had suggested, she undressed and lay down on the bed.

She was so tired after such a frightening night that she fell asleep and was only awakened when the maid brought her a can of hot water at seven o'clock.

Torilla got up quickly, washed, and put on a different gown from the one she had worn for travelling.

It was another cheap muslin dress which had been made by Abby and was certainly not the sort of evening-gown, she thought, that Sir Alexander would expect a guest of his to wear.

Abby had put a little frill of crisp white muslin round the neck and arranged it with narrow blue ribbons, with similar frills at the wrists to match.

The gown itself was pale blue and Torilla had in fact packed it for the journey because it was old and she was certain it would not be smart enough to wear at Fernleigh Park.

She wished now that she had one of her mother's gowns to wear, then she told herself she was being absurd.

Sir Alexander was obviously very grand and had only invited her to dinner because he was kind and he understood how frightened she had been the night before.

He would certainly not notice what anyone as insignificant as herself wore, and she only hoped she would not prove, as Abby had warned her, a bore by talking about things that did not appeal to him.

"I must be very careful to keep to subjects in which he is interested," she told herself.

She knew already that one thing they had in common was horses.

She brushed her fair hair until it shone, then she went down the stairs to find the landlord waiting for her at the foot of them.

"You are dining with Sir Alexander Abdy, I believe, Ma'am," he said.

Without waiting for Torilla to answer him, he went ahead of her and opened a door at the far end of the passage.

Torilla entered the room rather shyly.

It was not large, but at a quick glance she saw it was comfortable and attractive with an oak-beamed ceiling and walls decorated with ancient oak panelling.

There was a large open fireplace with a log fire.

A round table, covered with a spotless linen cloth, was set for two and there were several bottles of wine in a large ice-bucket.

Torilla had expected her host to look impressive since she had already been overwhelmed by the fit of his whipcord riding-coat, the intricate folds of his cravat, and the angle at which he wore his high-crowned hat on his dark hair.

But she had never known that any man could look as magnificent as the Marquis did in his evening-clothes, and for a moment she could only stare at him in admiration.

Then remembering her manners she curtseyed, and the Marquis bowed and indicated a chair by the fireside.

"Come and sit down, Miss Clifford, I hope you feel rested."

"I fell asleep," Torilla confessed.

"Then you will be looking forward to your dinner as much as I am," the Marquis said, "May I offer you a glass of madeira?"

"I have not ... drunk anything for ... two years," Torilla replied.

At home in Hertfordshire she had occasionally been allowed a few sips of madeira from her mother's glass.

"Then I will give you very little," the Marquis said with a smile.

He handed her a glass as he spoke and Torilla sipping the rich wine felt that it took her back to happy, golden days when there had been none of the pinching and saving that there was at Barrowfield.

Then her father and mother always drank wine at dinner and there had been plump chickens, well-roasted pigeons, and large joints of beef to eat.

Torilla told herself that she must obey Abby and not keep thinking of what lay behind her.

But as the landlord with two mob-capped maids brought in what seemed to her a gigantic meal she could not help remembering the children with their hollow cheeks and hungry eyes.

Resolutely she put such memories from her and enjoyed each dish that was offered, even though she could eat very little in comparison with her host.

"Tell me about yourself," the Marquis said as they were sampling a fine turbot which the Inn-keeper assured them was as fresh as if it had just jumped out of the sea.

"I would much rather talk about your horses, Sir," Torilla answered. "You said you had race-horses. Are you entering for any of the Classics this year?"

The diversion was successful.

The Marquis started talking of his ambition to win the Gold Cup at Ascot and discussed which owners were likely to defeat him in this object.

Then he found himself telling Torilla about his Arab thoroughbreds which had come from Syria, and the horses which his mother had admired from Hungary.

He talked at times almost indifferently, drawling his words while his eye-lids dropped lazily, but Torilla was not deceived. She knew his horses meant a great deal to him.

"I imagine you can ride well," he said a good deal later, bringing the conversation back to Torilla.

"I have not ridden for two years," she answered.

"Please tell me what horse you are entering for the St. Leger—then when September comes I can look for its name in the newspapers."

The Marquis accepted the change of subject, but he was astute enough to realise that the two years which Torilla had just mentioned had something significant about them.

At the same time, if she thought she was preventing him from questioning her, he was equally aware that she did not desire to talk about herself.

Because he had no wish to upset her he did not press the subject, but merely watched the different expressions which succeeded each other in her large and extraordinarily beautiful eyes.

As the meal drew to a close and the Marquis sat back with a glass of port in his hand, he thought it was the first time he could remember dining alone with a woman and talking entirely about himself.

Always those with whom he had spent so many idle hours had wanted to talk about themselves— granted, in connection with him—but they were never loath to express their feelings, their emotions, and indeed their ambitions extremely volubly and sometimes it seemed unceasingly.

"There is a mystery about this girl," he told himself.

As they moved from the table back to the fireplace, and the landlord, having set the decanter of port at the side of the Marquis's chair, withdrew from the room, he found himself curious.

"You are travelling south to be married or betrothed?" he enquired.

"No, nothing like that."

"You sound very positive. I am sure there are many men eager to pay their addresses to you."

Torilla smiled.

"Actually there is no-one."

He raised his eye-brows.

"Are there no men where you come from? Or are they all blind?"

Torilla blushed. The Marquis's eyes were amused as he watched the colour rise in her face, before he said in his deep voice:

"You are very beautiful, as you must be well aware when you look in your mirror."

Torilla looked into the fire and did not reply. But he saw her clasp and unclasp her fingers together and knew she was apprehensive.

"Where are you staying tomorrow night?" he asked in a different tone.

Torilla thought for a moment.

"I think it is the White Hart at Eaton Socom."

"Then I shall not be able to ask you to dine with me again," the Marquis said. "I turn off before I reach there."

He thought there was a shadow of disappointment in her eyes but was not sure.

"You must take care of yourself when I am not there to protect you," he went on, "although of course by rights, having rescued you twice, I should do so a third time."

"I hope not!" Torilla said quickly, then looked confused and added hastily: "I do not . . . mean that. I just mean that . . . accidents and . . . other adventures are disturbing and very . . . frightening."

"Of course they are," the Marquis agreed, "and that is why, as you well know, you should not be travelling alone."

"It could not be helped," she answered. "There was no-one who could come with me."

"No-one?" the Marquis questioned.

She shook her head, then as if she was afraid he would question her further she said:

"I think, Sir, as I have to rise very early tomorrow morning, and it is getting late, I should retire to bed."

She rose to her feet and the Marquis also rose.

He seemed to tower above her and she looked up at him thinking he was not only the most impressive but quite the most handsome man she had ever seen in her whole life.

Because she felt suddenly a little shy she said quickly:

"As I will not see you again, Sir, I want to thank you with all my ... heart for your ... kindness to me. If you had not ... been there last ... night ..."

She looked away from him with a little shudder and the Marquis said:

"But I was there, and perhaps, Torilla, one day we will meet again."

He held out his hand as he spoke, and she laid her fingers on it and his tightened over them.

It gave her a strange feeling and again because she felt shy she said:

"Thank you ... thank you ... I only wish I could ... express myself more ... eloquently."

"If you wish to express your gratitude," the Marquis said, "there is a very easy way to do so."

She looked up at him questioningly, not understanding what he meant.

He took his hand from hers and put his fingers under her chin.

It was impossible to move, impossible to think of what might happen, before his arms were round her and his lips came down on hers.

For a moment Torilla was too astonished even to breathe.

Then as his lips held her captive she thought she should struggle, that she must run away, but the touch of his mouth seemed to hypnotise her into immobility.

The warm insistence of it made her feel as if something live moved within her, rising through her body and her breasts and up into her throat.

It was a sensation so wonderful, so unlike anything she had ever known or dreamt of, that she ceased to think.

It grew in intensity until she felt as if she was no longer herself but a part of him, and everything that was beautiful, that she had ever known or longed for, seemed to be concentrated in the feeling he aroused in her.

He held her closer still, his arms imprisoning her, and yet she made no movement to escape.

Suddenly the wonder of his kiss became a rapture that was so intense, so ecstatic, that it seemed to pierce her with a dagger-like pain, yet it was a perfection and a glory that came from Heaven itself.

How long she was close against him, how long the kiss lasted, Torilla had no idea.

She only knew she was transported out of herself and into a place that had nothing to do with the world in which she lived and breathed.

It was as if her feet were no longer on the ground and she was flying through space, not a human being but a mythical spirit or nymph filled with magic. . . .

The Marquis raised his head and his eyes looked into hers.

She was trembling as she came back to earth with a thump and remembered who she was and why she was there.

Her face was radiant as she stared up at him, her lips parted, her breath coming quickly between them.

Then with a little inarticulate murmur, hardly knowing what she was doing, she turned and moved across the room.

She passed through the door, closing it behind her before she ran—or did she fly?—along the passage and up the stairs into the sanctuary of her bed-room.

Chapter Three

Torilla stepped out of the Stage-Coach when it reached Hatfield and saw that one of her uncle's carriages was waiting for her.

She also recognised the groom in his blue livery with silver crested buttons, who smiled as he raised his tall cockaded hat to say:

"Good-afternoon, Miss Torilla. Nice to see you again."

"And it is nice to see you, too, Ned," Torilla answered. "I am so relieved that you are here to meet me."

"Her Ladyship thought, Miss, you might not be arriving until tomorrow," Ned replied, "knowing how unpunctual the Coaches are."

He gave a disdainful glance at the unwieldy vehicle as he picked up Torilla's valise and carried it to where a closed landau drawn by two well-bred horses was waiting in the yard.

The coachman, whom Torilla also knew, greeted her, and she stepped into the comfortable carriage to sit back against the cushioned back while Ned collected her trunk.

It was just like old times, she thought, with attentive servants she had known since she was a child.

She wished Abby was with her to appreciate the quickness with which the guard of the Stage-Coach handed Ned her trunk. Then they were off towards the village of Fernford, which was two miles outside Hatfield.

All the time Torilla had been travelling for the last two days she had found it difficult to think of anything but Sir Alexander Abdy.

It had been impossible to sleep after he had kissed her and she had lain awake in the darkness, feeling the pressure of his lips still on hers and his arms enfolding her.

She had often wondered what it would be like to be kissed and now she thought to herself that never again could she be quite the same as she had been before.

When she listened to the fairy-stories her mother had told her and read them in books as she grew older, she had always felt there was something mystical and wonderful behind the ordinary things that were familiar.

She sensed that one day she would understand the yearning that was sometimes within herself and emotions which were inescapable.

When moonlight percolated between the branches of trees in great shafts of silver, or sunshine was dazzling on the stillness of water, she felt a response that was strange and yet exciting.

At other times she would be aroused by a butterfly hovering over the opening petals of a flower or when she heard music in the breeze blowing through the trees.

She had always felt then as if what she was trying to understand was just out of reach. She sensed it, felt it near her, and yet it was elusive and like a will o' the wisp she could not touch.

Suddenly she had captured it and had known it was hers at the touch of the Marquis's lips.

It had been so inexpressibly wonderful, and although her body responded to it she had known that the real glory of it was her mind.

She thought too that it was what she had often felt when she prayed and when she attended the Communion Service very early in the morning and the only light in the darkness of the Church was the candles on the altar.

Though she tried to explain to herself what she felt, it was beyond words: it was a secret but inseparable part of herself.

Shyly she thought that in a way last night she had also become a part of the man who had kissed her.

As the day passed and she spent another night in a Coaching Inn she thought perhaps she had imagined the whole thing.

Could there really be a man who looked like Sir Alexander Abdy? Who had such presence and such consequence, and could arouse in her feelings which made her quiver even to think of them?

'I shall never see him again,' she thought despairingly, and told herself that perhaps it was a good thing.

If she set aside the magic of what had happened, it came down to the fact that she had allowed a stranger, a man she had met by chance, to kiss her and she had made no attempt to struggle or free herself.

She had been completely submissive and captive in his arms.

That it was a wonder beyond wonders did not prevent her knowing that her mother would have been extremely shocked by her behaviour.

What was more, she herself could give no reasonable excuse for the manner in which she had behaved.

She could not bear to imagine what Abby would have thought had she accompanied her. However, if Abby had been there Sir Joscelyn would not have forced his way into her room and she would not have needed to be rescued.

Before she arrived at Fernleigh Hall, Torilla decided that she would never tell Abby, Beryl, or anyone else what had occurred.

It was a secret of which she was not ashamed because it had been almost a miracle of joy and she would not defame the memory of it by pretending she was sorry.

No-one would understand the inner consequence of what on the surface was only a reprehensible escapade.

The horses turned in through the small lodges which stood on either side of the huge wrought-iron gates surmounted by the Fernleigh Crest.

Then Torilla was driving between oak trees among which she and Beryl had played Hide and Seek when they were children, and she saw ahead of her the tall, red-brick mansion which had been built in the days of Queen Anne.

It was an attractive house and most people exclaimed at the splendour of its architecture, but to Torilla it was part of home.

She could hardly wait for the carriage door to be opened and the step to be let down before she sprang out.

Even as she did Beryl was there waiting for her at the top of the steps.

She put her arms round Torilla and the two cousins kissed each other affectionately while Beryl cried:

"Dearest, dearest Torilla! I have missed you! How glad I am to see you!"

"And I am happy to be here," Torilla answered with tears in her eyes.

"The Stage-Coach actually arrived on its proper day!" Beryl said. "I can hardly believe it, any more than I can believe that you are back. I have so much to tell you!"

She drew Torilla by the hand into the big Salon which overlooked the rose-garden at the back of the house.

Only as Torilla put up her hand to undo the ribbons of her bonnet and pull it off did she exclaim:

"Beryl! How lovely you have grown! You are much, much more beautiful than I remember!"

"I wanted you to think so," Beryl answered.

What Torilla had said was true.

Her cousin was indeed justly acclaimed as the most beautiful girl in England, and her admirers had not been exaggerating when they compared her to an English rose.

She had golden hair, not the colour of Torilla's but a vivid, gleaming sovereign gold. Her eyes were the colour of a thrush's egg, and her complexion was the pink and white of every woman's dreams.

She and Torilla were the same height and had as children been the same size, but now because Torilla had lived in the north on a starvation diet she was thinner than Beryl.

There were little hollows under her cheek-bones while Beryl's face was a smooth and well-filled oval.

With the crimson of her lips, which in fact owed not a little to artifice, the sparkle in her eyes, and the vivacity of the manner in which she talked which set her curls dancing, it was difficult for Torilla as for everyone else not to watch her in almost breathless admiration.

"You are so beautiful!" Torilla said again in awe-struck tones.

"And think how impressive I shall look when I am bedecked in all the gowns of my new trousseau," Beryl said, smiling.

She moved forward to kiss Torilla again on the cheek as she said:

"You will have to help me with it, dearest, or I shall never be ready on time. Oh, and that reminds me, there are two more names I must write down on the wedding-list."

With a quick movement like a little humming-bird she sped across the Salon to the *secretaire* to pick up a white quill-pen and start writing.

As she did so she said over her shoulder:

"I know someone will be forgotten and will therefore become an enemy for life, and that is why I am making a list as I think of them."

Torilla put down her bonnet before she replied:

"You must show it to me; then I can ask you about all the friends I used to know but who I am afraid will have forgotten me by now."

"Captain and Mrs. Chalmers," Beryl said aloud as she inscribed their names.

"I remember them," Torilla exclaimed. "She was a very sweet woman, but I always thought he was rather aggressive."

Beryl did not reply and after a moment Torilla said:

"That reminds me of another soldier. How is Rodney?"

Beryl was suddenly very still, but Torilla did not notice.

"It will be fun to see him again," she went on. "Do you remember how he used to tease us? Like when he took away the ladder and we had to stay in the hayloft in the stables for over an hour before we were rescued!"

She gave a little laugh.

"I am sure if anyone is jealous about your being married it will be Rodney."

Then as Beryl did not reply, Torilla sensed that something was wrong.

"What is it?" she asked in a low voice.

"Rodney is dead!"

As she spoke, Beryl rose from the *secretaire* and walked towards one of the long french windows opening onto the garden.

"Dead?" Torilla repeated in astonishment. "Oh, Beryl, I had no idea! No-one told me. How could he have died?"

She was silent until Beryl said:

"He was killed in France."

"But the war was over when Papa and I left here,"

Torilla said. "Do you not remember how excited we were when we heard that Paris had surrendered?"

There was a pause before Beryl answered:

"The Duke of Wellington did not know that the Allied Forces had taken Paris and that the war was really over."

"We knew that Rodney's Regiment had entered France at St.-Jean-de-Luz," Torilla said almost as if she was speaking to herself.

"They fought their way as far as Toulouse," Beryl said in a strangled voice. "Of course we did not learn until much, much later that Marshal Soult was convinced that Toulouse was impregnable."

"And so the Duke of Wellington attacked it," Torilla said as if she knew the end of the story.

"There were very heavy . . . losses," Beryl went on with tears in her voice. "The newspapers reported that nearly five thousand of our troops were killed and . . . Rodney was . . . among them."

"Oh . . . I am sorry, Beryl. I am so very, very sorry," Torilla cried. "I had no idea, and you never told me in your letters."

"The Marsdens heard nothing until after Christmas," Beryl explained. "Then they were told that . . . Rodney was not amongst the . . . survivors of the battle."

"I can hardly believe it!" Torilla whispered.

Rodney Marsden had been so much a part of her and Beryl's childhood.

His father, Squire Marsden, had an Estate which matched with the Earl's, and Rodney, although he was three years older than Beryl, was, like the two cousins, an only child.

Inevitably he spent his holidays from school in their company.

Because the Earl was fond of him he allowed him to shoot ducks on the lakes, pigeons and rabbits in the woods, and occasionally when he grew older he accompanied his father pheasant and partridge shooting.

Squire Marsden had some good horses, especially hunters, and Rodney appointed himself to lead Beryl and Torilla in the hunting-field.

He was also their dancing partner at the parties all their parents gave at Christmastime and Torilla thought of him as if he were the brother she would have loved to have.

It was only now that she had learnt that he was dead that she knew how much she had looked forward to seeing him again.

She moved across the Salon, put her arms round Beryl, and said softly:

"The only consolation is that was the way Rodney would have . . . wanted to . . . die. He was so proud to be in the Army."

For a moment Beryl clung to Torilla, then she moved away and said in a different voice:

"I have taught myself not to think about him. When somebody is dead there is nothing one can do, and tears are extremely unbecoming!"

It sounded a frivolous remark, but Torilla knew because she loved her cousin that Beryl was hiding her real feelings.

Because she understood that some things were too poignant to be discussed she replied lightly:

"Tell me about your engagement. You know, Beryl, it is so like you, but you forgot to tell me your future husband's name."

"Wait until you see him, then you will be really impressed," Beryl replied. "Oh, Torilla, I am so lucky —the luckiest girl in the world! Everyone has tried to capture Gallen, every single woman in the country —and a great many more who were already married."

Her lips were smiling as she went on:

"They have tried every sort of bait on the biggest fish in the Social Pool, but—clever me—I am the one who has caught him!"

The way she spoke jarred a little on Torilla but she said aloud:

"I am sure where you are concerned, dearest, he was happy to be caught."

"It is the triumph of my life," Beryl continued, "a *grande finale* to my career as an 'Incomparable.' You have heard that the Prince Regent called me that?"

"You told me so in several of your letters," Torilla replied.

"I could not tell you half the things I wanted to," Beryl said. "I hate letter-writing. Besides, I never have enough time."

She twirled her elaborately embroidered skirt round her as she exclaimed:

"I am such a success! I do not know where to begin to relate it all. I am asked to every party, every Assembly, every Ball! No-one would dare to give an entertainment without me!"

Torilla laughed.

"You are boasting just as you used to do when you drew the best prize out of the Bran-dip at Christmas. I can see you now as you ran round the room crying:

" 'Look at me! I have the biggest box of bonbons! Am I not clever?' "

"And that is exactly what I have now," Beryl answered, "for no-one could imagine a bigger bonbon than Gallen. He is a Corinthian, a Buck, a Beau, and the Prince Regent dotes on him!"

She paused for breath but before Torilla could speak she went on:

"I cannot begin to tell you how rich he is. Papa thinks he is the wealthiest man in the whole country. His Castle in Huntingdonshire is just made for entertaining."

She made an excited gesture with her hands as she continued:

"I shall be the most important and certainly the most influential hostess in the whole of the *Beau Monde!* What is more, I shall be covered in diamonds!"

Torilla laughed again.

"Oh, Beryl, you are ridiculous! But you are not telling me what I want to know."

"What is that?"

"Are you very . . . very much . . . in love?"

There was a little silence before Beryl said:

"My dear Torilla, love as we used to talk about it when we were children is something felt by peasants."

Torilla looked at her to see if she was serious before she asked:

"What are you . . . saying to me?"

"I am saying that Gallen and I will deal very well together because we like the same things, we are Social Stars in the same firmament, and we both know how to behave like civilised people."

"Then . . . you are not . . . in love with him?" Torilla exclaimed. "In which case, why are you marrying him?"

"Why am I marrying him?" Beryl echoed. "I have just told you, he is the richest, most important man in England. What more could any girl ask?"

"But . . . Beryl . . ." Torilla faltered, an anxious expression in her eyes. "When we used to talk about love and when you first made your début we both swore we would never marry unless we fell in love."

"It is what I intended to do," Beryl said quietly, "but it has not worked out like that."

"And you think you will be happy . . . without it?" Torilla asked.

"But of course I will be happy with Gallen," Beryl replied. "I shall have everything I want—everything!"

"And he loves you?" Torilla asked. "He must; otherwise there is no reason for him to marry you."

Beryl gave her one of her puckish looks.

"Gallen wants a son and heir. Who would not, with all those possessions to be inherited? I also have a feeling, Torilla, although of course he has never mentioned it to me, that he is escaping from the rather ardent attentions of a very persistent widow."

Torilla sat down on the sofa.

"I am not happy about this, Beryl."

"You sound exactly like one of our Governesses," Beryl said. "Heavens, that reminds me, I had forgotten Miss Dawson! She must be invited to the wedding."

She sped back to the *secretaire* and as she sat down Torilla said:

"You have not told me yet the name of your future husband. I have learnt he is Christened 'Gallen,' but he must have another name."

"He is the Marquis of Havingham," Beryl replied.

She had her back to her cousin and therefore did not see the incredulous look in Torilla's eyes being replaced by one of sheer horror.

For a moment it seemed as if she could hardly breathe, then she ejaculated in a strangled voice:

"No . . . no! It is not . . . possible!"

"I knew you would be impressed," Beryl said. "Even in the unfashionable north you must have heard of the Marquis of Havingham. Now you will understand why I am so excited about my marriage."

Torilla drew in her breath.

She could not believe what Beryl had told her was true. She could not credit that her cousin, whom she loved and with whom she had been brought up, was to marry a man she loathed and hated with every fibre of her being.

How could she possibly explain to Beryl, who was so excited by the thought of getting married, that her intended husband was a cruel monster, a man who was responsible for the deaths of children, for maiming their mothers and turning their fathers into louts?

The image of Barrowfield swam in front of her eyes.

The ghastly squalor of the dirty, grimy houses,

the heaps of burning coal obscuring even the brightness of the sky, as did the forges and engine chimneys roaring and puffing on every side.

She could see in her imagination, as her father had often depicted to her, the trappers, children of five years of age, spending as many as sixteen hours a day crouching in solitude in a small dark hole.

Others would push or pull coal-trucks along the tunnels. The pumps in the Havingham mine were so out-of-date and so ineffectual that the children would be standing ankle-deep in water for twelve hours on end.

Her father would come home at night to pour out his grievances against the owner of the mine, saying in exhausted tones, because he had not even the energy left to express himself, how diabolical the conditions were.

"The place is not safe," he had said often enough, and when Torilla had asked despairingly:

"Cannot anything be done, Papa?" her father had merely shrugged his shoulders and replied:

"Who cares? Certainly not the Marquis of Havingham!"

Everything she had seen and heard of the misery, dirt, and degradation of Barrowfield flashed through Torilla's mind.

Her first impulse was to describe to Beryl what was happening in Barrowfield and urge that whoever else she married it must not be the Marquis of Havingham.

Then almost as if she stood beside her she could hear Abby warning her against boring people in the south with their troubles.

"They'll not understand," Abby had said, and Torilla knew that was true.

Before she went with her father to Barrowfield she would not have understood, and she doubted if even her mother, compassionate, sympathetic, and understanding though she had been, could have visualised the horrors that existed there.

With what was almost a superhuman effort she said nothing.

As Beryl rose from the *secretaire* she suggested:

"Let us go upstairs, dearest. I want to show you some of the things I have bought for my trousseau. There are few of them as yet but we will go to London next week and spend a fortune on the most magnificent gowns that Bond Street can provide."

As she spoke she walked towards Torilla, but when she reached her she said with a note of concern in her voice:

"You look pale, dearest. I expect you are tired after that long journey, and it is not surprising."

"I am a little . . . tired," Torilla managed to reply.

She was silent as Beryl took her upstairs and she found she was sleeping in the room she had always occupied when they were young.

Sometimes her father and mother would go away and it was taken as a matter of course that Torilla should stay at Fernleigh Hall, just as whenever it suited the Earl and the Countess, Beryl came to them.

On such occasions the two girls would conspire together to carry out some daring exploit, such as climbing the hay-stacks or swimming in the lake after they should have been in bed and asleep.

In consequence, the room next door to Beryl's bed-chamber was always known as "Miss Torilla's Room," and now it was waiting for her, the silk curtains drawn back from the windows which looked over the sun-kissed lake.

For a moment Torilla saw only a blackened countryside without trees or shrubs, with the slum of the men, women, and children who lived in it almost as black as the coal they handled.

Then deliberately she made Beryl talk of her trousseau and later in the evening of her wedding.

Tentatively because she was so afraid of saying too much Torilla asked hesitatingly:

"You do not . . . think, dearest, that if you . . . waited a little longer you would find someone you would . . . love with all your . . . heart?"

She saw the expression on Beryl's face and added quickly:

"You look like the Princess in a fairy-story. I want you to find your Prince Charming."

"Wait until you see Gallen," Beryl said complacently. "He is exactly the Prince Charming we talked about when you used to sit on my bed and we wondered who we would marry."

She smiled as she went on:

"I always envisaged myself a Queen or a Princess. In fact I have found the next best thing in Gallen, who is far more important than most Princes and certainly far more solvent than the Prince Regent!"

"That, I imagine, would not be difficult," Torilla answered. "Even I have heard of the mountain of debts which His Royal Highness owes!"

"I should hate to be so much in debt," Beryl said. "As it is, I shall find it very difficult to spend even a part of Gallen's fortune."

She stretched her arms above her head as she exclaimed:

"That is why I intend to have a trousseau that will astonish everybody, and you will benefit."

Torilla knew what Beryl was going to say.

"I intend to discard every stitch that I own now," her cousin went on, "every single thing, and they are all yours."

"Thank you, dearest," Torilla said. "It is very, very kind of you."

At the same time, she could not help wondering what use she would have for Beryl's lovely gowns in Barrowfield.

The material would be too fragile to be cut up and used for miners' wives and their children, although she was quite certain her father would have expected her to do just that if it were possible.

"I shall have new fans, new reticules, new sun-shades, new slippers, and new gloves!"

Beryl flung herself back against the soft cushions on the sofa as she went on:

"I am not being extravagant, Torilla, but sensible! Gallen admires smart, elegant women. In fact I am the only girl, if that is what you can call me, in whom he has ever shown the slightest interest."

She sat up again, rested her chin on her hand, and said reflectively:

"I shall have to be very sophisticated to please him, and quite frankly, Torilla, he will be tricky as a husband."

"What do you mean by that?" Torilla asked.

"Judging from his past history, he not only has an eye for a horse but also for a pretty woman."

"Are you really expecting him to be ... unfaithful?" Torilla asked in a shocked little voice.

"For goodness' sake, Torilla, grow up!" Beryl replied. "Of course Gallen will have his flirtations, as I shall have mine, but I have to be very careful that no-one supplants me. I know only too well what women are like where a man as rich and important as Gallen is concerned."

"Supplants you?" Torilla repeated. "Do you mean he would run away with another woman?"

"No, of course not!" Beryl said. "People in our world do not cause scandals of that sort ... not unless they are crazy."

She spoke rather sharply. Then as she saw the expression on Torilla's face she said more gently:

"You always were out of touch with reality, Torilla. What I am trying to say is that if a man is really bored with his wife he can make life very unpleasant for her."

Beryl's voice was hard as she continued:

"She can be left in the country for months on

end with no-one but the children to talk to, or he can keep her short of money like that odious Lord Boreham!"

She paused as if remembering His Lordship's parsimony, then finished:

"In fact there are a thousand ways that a wife can be made to feel unwanted and miserable!"

She rose to her feet as she continued firmly:

"I have every intention of keeping Gallen at my side, but I am not going to pretend it will be easy."

"If he . . . loved you," Torilla said tentatively, "it might be very . . . different."

"He is fond enough of me," Beryl answered, "and quite frankly I do not think Gallen has ever been in love with anyone except himself and his horses."

Again she looked at Torilla's expression and laughed.

"Do not look so worried, dearest! I shall have my fun too. Lord Newall is crazily, wildly in love with me. Do you know, the other night he produced a pistol and declared that either I must let him kiss me or he would blow his brains out!"

"Did he mean it?" Torilla asked breathlessly.

"I did not take the risk of finding out!" Beryl replied mischievously.

"You mean . . . you let him . . . kiss you?"

"Of course I did, and very pleasant it was, if you want to know."

Torilla opened her lips to expostulate. Then she asked herself how she could criticise Beryl after what had happened on her way south.

"We had better go to bed," Beryl said. "Papa is coming home tomorrow and after that the balloon will go up!"

"What do you mean by that?" Torilla enquired.

"Mama insisted on Papa being with her in London when the announcement of my engagement appeared in the *Gazette*. They will have been receiving congratulations all today, and tomorrow, make no mistake about it, the hordes of callers will arrive here."

Beryl gave a little laugh.

"It will amuse me to see the people who have criticised me during the past few years now fawning at my feet. They will not wish to quarrel with the future Marchioness of Havingham!"

The two girls went up the stairs arm in arm and Beryl came with Torilla into her bed-room.

"I am longing to talk to you," she said, "but I am sure, dearest, that you are tired, and I must have my 'beauty sleep.' "

She glanced at her reflection in the mirror as she spoke as if to reassure herself that it was really unnecessary. Then she said:

"I expect Gallen also will arrive tomorrow, and then you will see that all I have told you about him is not exaggerated."

She kissed Torilla, then opened the communicating door between the two rooms.

"Good-night, my dear, good little Torilla," she said. "I am sorry I have shocked you! We must not forget your bridesmaid's gown when we go to London. I want you to look very attractive, but I warn you, I brook no rivals!"

"As though anyone could rival you," Torilla said as she had said to Abby.

"You would be surprised how many people try," Beryl retorted as she shut the door behind her.

* * *

The following day Torilla found that Beryl had not exaggerated when she had said that the "balloon" would go up.

From early in the morning grooms arrived with invitations, letters of congratulation, bouquets of flowers, and presents.

Beryl was as excited about them as she had been with her Christmas gifts as a child.

"Read the flattering things old Lord Godolphin says!" she exclaimed, thrusting a letter into Torilla's hand. "He is a ghastly old hypocrite. He has hated me ever since I was fifteen when he tried to kiss me and I punched him in the stomach."

"It is certainly a very pleasant letter," Torilla said quietly.

"Toadying old fool!" Beryl replied.

The presents were disappointing.

"That makes three silver entrée dishes already!" Beryl sighed. "You would think people would realise that Gallen has the best family silver in England, most of which dates back to the reign of Charles II."

She pushed the entrée dishes aside disdainfully.

"I suppose we can always use them for the dogs," she laughed.

There were a large number of people to add to the wedding-list whom Beryl had forgotten.

When the Earl of Fernleigh walked into the Salon it was to find not only lists scattered all over the floor, but also pieces of paper, boxes, presents, and several bouquets of flowers.

"Hello, Papa!" Beryl exclaimed casually.

Torilla scrambled to her feet and kissed her uncle affectionately.

"It is nice to see you again, Torilla," the Earl said with a note of genuine affection in his voice.

"It is lovely to be back, Uncle Hector."

"Surely by now your father is tired of burying himself in the wilds of nowhere?" the Earl suggested.

"He is working too hard, Uncle Hector."

"Then tell him to come back here. The Vicar of Wheathampstead is retiring soon. It is a good incumbency and I am quite prepared to add a few hundred to the stipend if your father will take it on."

"That is very kind of you, Uncle Hector."

"Tell him it is his for the asking," the Earl said. "I have missed you, Torilla, and you are a good influence on Beryl, which is more than some people are."

He walked from the room as he spoke and Beryl made a little grimace.

"What does he mean by that?" Torilla asked.

"He hates most of my friends," Beryl replied. "He thinks they are fast and improper, which indeed they are, but they are certainly more amusing than the old fuddy-duddies whom Papa likes to entertain."

"Do you really ... like all the people you ... meet at Carlton House?" Torilla asked a little hesitantly.

Beryl smiled at her.

"Some of them are fantastic!" she said. "You wonder where the Prince could find such extraordinary people. But the worst are the members of the aristocracy, like the Marquis of Queensbury, who is absolutely famous for his amorous indiscretions!"

She laughed at the expression on Torilla's face and added:

"The wicked Barrymore brothers are horrors of the worst description; you would be appalled at the things they do."

"I think I would be ... frightened of people like that," Torilla said.

"It will be amusing to see what effect they have on you," Beryl laughed. "You will meet them all when we go to London next week."

Torilla looked at her questioningly and Beryl went on:

"I have just decided, Torilla, that I shall present you to the *Beau Monde*. It will not only be fun to see what you think of it, but also to watch what they think of you! I do not believe any of them have ever met anybody who is really good!"

"You make me embarrassed," Torilla exclaimed.

"It is true," Beryl said. "You are good—you always were—while I am the opposite. I want to be bad.

Not wicked like the Barrymores, but just bad enough to enjoy all the things I ought not to."

"You are not bad!" Torilla contradicted loyally. "And, dearest, when you are married it will be very different."

Beryl did not answer and Torilla suddenly had the uncomfortable feeling that, on the contrary, perhaps it would be worse.

If the Marquis was as wicked as she thought him to be, would he not drive Beryl, who had always been impulsive, into doing things that she might afterwards regret?

Torilla suddenly felt very apprehensive, then she shied away from her own thoughts.

Beryl talked a lot of nonsense, but undoubtedly she would continue to be just as sweet, kind, and generous as before, although, it was to be admitted, she was susceptible to flattery.

'And who could blame her,' Torilla wondered, 'when she is so beautiful . . . so amazingly beautiful.'

She remembered her mother saying once:

"Beryl is like a picture by Reubens—all brilliant colours. You, my darling, are an exquisite water-colour which creeps into one's soul so that you find it difficult to think of any other painting as being so lovely."

Torilla thought at the time that her mother was only consoling her because Beryl attracted so much more attention than she did.

Now she thought that Beryl was in fact, with her gaiety, her sparkle, and her vivacity, very like a brilliant, breathtaking picture by a great master.

Then as if she wished to change the subject Torilla asked:

"What shall we do with all these flowers? The lilies are perfect!"

She picked up a big bunch of them as she spoke and looked down at them, their fragrance seeming to have a mystical quality about it.

"You had better have those put in your bed-room

if you like them so much," Beryl replied, "but throw the rest away. There are too many flowers in the house as it is."

"Oh, no! You must not do that!" Torilla exclaimed.

She had always thought of flowers as being alive and liable to suffer as much as human beings could, and she hated it when the servants forgot to water them or they were thrown away before they were dead.

"I will see to them," she said, knowing that Beryl was not listening.

There was the sound of voices in the Hall and her cousin started to her feet.

"It is Gallen!" she exclaimed. "I thought he would come today! Oh, how exciting! Now you can see him."

She rushed across the room to pull open the door.

"Gallen! Gallen!" Torilla heard her exclaim. "How wonderful that you are here! I have been so looking forward to seeing you!"

A man's deep voice replied, but Torilla could not hear what he said.

Standing with the lilies in her arms, she was steeling herself for the moment which made her whole body feel tense. The horror the Marquis of Havingham evoked in her was like a live coal burning in her breast.

She hated him—she hated him so intensely that she thought if it was within her power she would strike him dead.

Last night when she had gone to bed she had prayed with a fervency she had never used before that something would prevent him from marrying Beryl.

How could she allow anyone she loved to marry a man who would commit such crimes against human beings as the Marquis had committed against the miners and their families?

She had always pictured him as fat and gross with lines of debauchery under his eyes.

She had imagined him sitting at a table weighed down with food and drinking red wine which was the

colour of the blood of those who sweated for him in
the darkness and dust of his filthy pit.

"How can any man be so bestial, so heartless?"
she asked herself.

The miners of Barrowfield were not only over-
worked but also underpaid, and she knew that they
were also tricked by the Overseer, who she supposed
had been appointed by the Marquis.

There were many ways in which the miners could
suffer so that those in charge of them could line their
pockets.

There were always wage deductions to pay for the
candles and the powder they used. An Overseer could,
if he chose, make the men buy candles from him for
one and a half or twopence above the market price.

This, Torilla had learnt from her father, was
what happened in the Havingham mine.

Payment for broken tools also reduced a man's
wages and the Overseer could demand a sum far in ex-
cess of the current market value of the goods.

The Vicar had been very explicit about the iniqui-
ty of this.

"They are charging one shilling for a shovel
shaft," he had said furiously one day to Torilla, "and
a peggy shaft costs sixpence here, although hitherto it
had cost twopence."

"Can nothing be done?" Torilla had asked once
again.

"Who cares if the men are cheated?" the Vicar
had asked scathingly.

Certainly not the wealthy Marquis, a man who
had Castles and houses, servants and race-horses, and
was now taking an expensive wife.

She heard the voices in the Hall drawing nearer to
the door and she braced herself for a contact with the
man she thought of as "the Devil."

She tightened her hold on the great bunches of
lilies which she still held in her arms and her eyes were

wide and dark in her pale face as she waited. Then she could not look, it was so frightening.

Beryl came in first.

"Here is Gallen, dearest Torilla, and now you can meet him!"

A man followed Beryl into the Salon, his polished Hessian boots reflecting the furniture and the chaos of paper, flowers, and presents on the floor.

With an effort Torilla raised her eyes, then her heart turned a double somersault in her breast.

She thought that the ceiling fell down on her head and the whole room whirled round her!

It was not the Marquis of Havingham who followed Beryl, but Sir Alexander Abdy!

Chapter Four

Torilla walked in through the gates of the Park and saw the ground beneath the oak trees covered with a golden carpet of daffodils.

It was early in the morning, and she had been to the seven o'clock Communion in the little village Church where she had been Christened.

There were only half a dozen other people at the Service, and when it was over Torilla had gone to the Church-yard to stand beside her mother's grave under a yew tree.

She looked down at the plain headstone and found it hard to believe that her mother, whom she had loved so deeply, and who had always been so sweet and understanding, had left her.

Then she had told herself that was not true.

Her mother's spirit was alive, and wherever she might be her thoughts and her love would always be with her father and herself.

"Help me, Mama, to do what I can for Beryl," Torilla said in her heart. "Knowing how he treats the people in Barrowfield, how can I let her marry the Marquis?"

She did not include it in her prayers, but she knew, if she was honest, that her feelings about the Marquis were conflicting and confused.

How, when she knew him to be a monster of cal-

lousness and cruelty, could he also be the man who
had evoked such a divine rapture within her that even
to think of his kiss still made her quiver?

Ever since he arrived at the Hall she had found it
impossible to look at him or to meet his eyes.

When he had entered the Salon and she had curtseyed automatically without any conscious volition on
her part, her heart had been beating so furiously in her
breast that she had thought he must hear it.

Her eye-lashes were very dark against her pale
cheeks. Then as she rose she heard him say:

"Delightful to meet you, Miss Clifford!"

She told herself then that her feelings against him
were no less vehement than before his arrival, and yet
there was an undoubted tremor in her voice as she
answered politely:

"Thank you . . . My Lord."

Beryl was quite unaware that there was any ten-
sion between the Marquis and her cousin.

"Come and look at our presents, Gallen," she had
said, pulling him by the arm. "They are quite nauseat-
ing, and the only thing we can do is give them away to
other unfortunate couples in the future."

As she took the Marquis towards the untidy mess
of presents, letters, and paper, Torilla, still clenching
the lilies against her, had escaped.

How could it be possible, she asked herself as she
ran upstairs, that the Marquis was Sir Alexander Abdy,
the man whom, despite every resolution, she had
dreamt about every night since she had last seen him
and thought about a thousand times a day?

"I hate him! I hate him!" she told herself over
and over again as if the mere words were a talisman
which would erase the memory of that magical, inexpressibly wonderful kiss.

She had been very quiet at dinner that night, but
neither Beryl nor her uncle noticed because they were
so busy talking.

The Earl had plenty to relate about the congratulations he had received in London after the *Gazette* had published the announcement of his daughter's betrothal.

At the same time, Beryl was quite determined that the Marquis's attention should not wander long from herself.

She was looking extremely beautiful in a gown which matched the colour of her eyes and wearing a necklace of aquamarines which, set with diamonds, sparkled with every movement she made.

She made the Marquis laugh several times and Torilla thought that no man could fail to be in love with anyone so alluring. But she was so afraid of meeting the Marquis's eyes that she did not look at him.

Only as dinner was drawing to a close did the Marquis ask unexpectedly as Beryl was talking of the wedding:

"What part is Miss Clifford to play in all these celebrations?"

It was a question that made Torilla start and the colour rose in her cheeks.

"Torilla is to be my only bridesmaid," Beryl replied. "I have not had time, Gallen, to tell you how much she means in my life. We were brought up together."

"Yes, indeed," the Earl interposed, "and we have all missed you very much, Torilla, since you left us for the far north."

"I have missed you, too, Uncle Hector," Torilla said in a low voice.

"Well, you are back now," the Earl smiled, "and at least we shall have you with us until Beryl is married."

"That reminds me . . ." Beryl exclaimed, and she was chattering again about the wedding-ceremony and the huge number of people who had to be accommodated at the Reception.

As soon as dinner was over and the gentlemen came into the Salon, Torilla had slipped away once again to the peace and quietness of her bed-room.

She told herself that she was being tactful because Beryl would wish to be alone with the Marquis.

But she knew in her heart that it was really because she was afraid of being near him and because she felt as if everything he was, said, and did was whirling round in her brain until she was almost driven mad by the complexity of it.

She had been unable to sleep, and almost as soon as it was light she knew that because it was Sunday she must go to Church.

She did not suppose the times of the Services would have changed greatly from when her father was the incumbent of the small Parish.

He always insisted on a very early Communion-Service for those who had work to do later on in the day.

When Torilla entered the nave of the small grey stone Norman Church she felt as if she were a child again and everything was right with the world.

Her father and mother were at the Vicarage and the God in whom she had always believed so devoutly was here to listen to her prayers.

It had been hard to believe that the same God watched over Barrowfield.

Sometimes when she heard the horrors of what happened in the mine she had felt there was no longer a merciful Lord who her father had always said cared for all His children, wherever they might be.

The days here were so much warmer than in the north. The sun was rising golden in the sky as Torilla, walking beneath the oak trees whose branches met over her head, pulled off her bonnet.

'How happy Beryl and I were,' she thought, 'when as children we used to run and hide behind the trees.'

She could remember herself hoping that Beryl or Rodney would not find her, but she had always been too impatient to wait quietly and they would see her peeping out and rush upon her with whoops of joy.

If she ran away it made it even more exciting.

She remembered all three of them running over the soft grass until they were tired, to fling themselves down by the side of the lake, panting with breathlessness and laughter.

Sometimes Rodney would tease them and threaten to throw them both into the still water.

'Now Rodney is dead, and Beryl and I are grown up,' Torilla thought with a little pang, 'and there are problems . . . terrible problems for both of us.'

As if her very words conjured up the man she was trying to avoid, she saw at that moment the Marquis riding up the drive towards her.

Instinctively she wanted to hide herself and she moved quickly behind one of the great oak trunks to stand with her back against it, hoping he had not seen her.

She stood, listening, thinking she would hear his horse's hoofs on the gravel. But he must have moved onto the grass verge, for so unexpectedly that it made her jump he appeared and looked down at her from the back of a black stallion.

"Are you communing with nature, Torilla, or avoiding me?" he asked.

She did not answer and he dismounted. She felt herself tremble as leaving his horse free he came to stand beside her.

She did not look at him but at the stallion who bent his head to crop the grass.

"I am waiting for an answer to my question," the Marquis said in an amused tone.

Torilla tried to look at him but felt her eye-lashes flicker and asked rather inconsequentially:

"Will your . . . horse not . . . wander . . . away?"

"Sullivan belongs to me," the Marquis replied. "I brought him with me yesterday when I arrived. He comes when I call him."

Torilla said nothing and after a moment he said:

"I have answered your question, now it is your turn."

"I . . . I was just walking home from . . . Church."

"You have been to Church?" the Marquis asked with a slight note of surprise in his voice. Then he added:

"Of course, it is Sunday. What did you pray for?"

"I prayed for Beryl," Torilla answered truthfully.

As she spoke she moved forward, walking through the grass, hoping that the Marquis would leave her alone.

But he walked beside her and as she kept her head down she was conscious of the brilliant polish on his Hessian boots, and at the same time she knew without raising her eyes that he was looking at her.

"You were surprised to see me?" the Marquis asked after they had walked for a few moments in silence.

"Y-yes."

"I was astonished to see you," he answered. "Why did you not tell me where you were going?"

"You . . . did not . . . ask me."

"I was sure you did not wish to answer my questions. In fact I knew you were deliberately avoiding them," the Marquis replied.

She was surprised that he should be so perceptive.

"When I came into the Salon and saw you standing there with the lilies in your arms," he went on, "I thought you must be a figment of my imagination."

He paused before he continued:

"I had been thinking about you all day; in fact ever since I left the George and Dragon it was impossible to think of anything else."

Torilla told herself she must be dreaming, that he could not be saying such things to her. Then he asked:

"I gather you have not told Beryl that we met before?"

"N-no!"

"Why not?"

There was a pause before Torilla said hesitatingly: "I . . . I would not . . . wish to . . . hurt her."

"Do you think she would be hurt?" the Marquis enquired. "I rather doubt it."

Again there was that mocking note in his voice.

"It was . . . wrong and quite indefensible," Torilla said slowly, "that you should behave as you . . . did when you had just become . . . engaged to Beryl."

"It was you who wished to thank me more eloquently than could be said in words," the Marquis reminded her.

This was true, but Torilla thought angrily that he was trying to put all the blame on her.

"And after all," he continued, "was it really such a heinous sin, if that is how you are thinking of it now?"

It had not seemed a sin, Torilla thought, but the most wonderful, perfect thing that had ever happened to her.

But he was engaged to Beryl, and she knew that if she were in her cousin's position she would think it intolerably disloyal of the man she was to marry to kiss somebody else.

"What you feel and what Beryl feels are two very different things," the Marquis remarked.

He had read her thoughts and Torilla looked at him in a startled fashion.

"I make no apologies, no excuses for what happened," the Marquis said in a low voice.

It was impossible for her to take her eyes from his. Then with an effort Torilla remembered who he was and turned her face away.

"When I came into the Salon yesterday," the Marquis said, "I saw you look at me and I knew that for one second you were glad to see me. Then your eyes changed and you looked at me with what I can only describe as hatred. Why?"

Torilla drew in her breath.

How could he have watched her so closely? She wondered. How could he be so sensitive to what she was feeling?

This was the Marquis of Havingham, the man whose callousness and brutality were responsible for such crimes against nature that she had wished him dead ever since she had gone to Barrowfield.

Distraught by her feeling, she found they had walked to where in the Park a tree had fallen down.

Without really thinking what she was doing, Torilla sat down on the trunk, and the Marquis, with his eyes on her face, sat beside her.

His horse had followed them and now once again the stallion put his head down, seeking the young grass.

"I want an explanation, Torilla," the Marquis said. "Your eyes are very expressive, so it will be difficult for you to keep any secrets from me."

"I would . . . rather you did not . . . question me."

"I knew that was what you felt when we dined together," the Marquis replied. "But the situation has now changed. What you feel now has something to do with me personally, has it not?"

"Y-yes."

The monosyllable seemed to be drawn from between Torilla's lips.

"And it is not simply that you are angry because I kissed you?"

"I was not . . . angry," Torilla faltered. "I was only . . . sh-shocked after I realised when you came here . . . yesterday . . . that Sir Alexander Abdy was you!"

"But there is something else as well," the Marquis insisted.

Torilla did not speak and after a moment he went on:

"You said you had been praying for Beryl in

the Church. Did you pray that she should not marry me?"

Again Torilla was startled that he should be almost clairvoyant where she was concerned, and because he seemed to mesmerise her into telling him the truth, she said in a low voice:

"Yes . . . I did . . . pray for that."

"I wonder which of my many sins and indiscretions have caught up with me. There are quite a number which I imagine you, of all people, would find unpalatable."

Now he was speaking mockingly and, Torilla felt, laughing at her.

As if she felt it was intolerable that they should go on with this conversation, she rose from the fallen tree.

"I wish to go . . . back to the Hall, My Lord."

The Marquis did not rise, he merely put out his hand and caught her wrist.

"Not until you have told me what I want to know."

Torilla felt herself quiver at his touch.

She did not understand why, but she felt almost as if little shafts of lightning shot through her body because his fingers were touching her skin.

"Tell me, Torilla," the Marquis said. "You cannot leave me in suspense, and I trust you not to lie to me."

"You will . . . not like the . . . truth."

"I am not afraid to hear it."

She tried to pull her wrist free but the Marquis held her captive, and now looking away from him to where the morning sun was glinting on the lake she said in a low voice that he could hardly hear:

"I come from . . . Barrowfield!"

"Barrowfield?" the Marquis repeated.

She knew by the questioning tone in his voice that the name seemed to mean nothing to him.

He might have forgotten, or it might be a place that he found it hard to connect with her.

Whatever the reason, it swept away Torilla's hesitation and timidity, and the anger and hatred she had felt was stronger than the feeling the Marquis evoked in her by his touch.

"Yes, Barrowfield," she said, and now her voice was strong. "It is in Yorkshire, My Lord, and it is a filthy, foul, squalid place because the people who live there work in the Havingham mine!"

She drew in her breath.

"Does that mean nothing to you? Well, let me tell you what it means to the miners and their families."

She turned round as she spoke and now the Marquis released her wrist.

"Do you know that your pit is unsafe?" Torilla asked. "Do you know there are accidents practically every month, when if the men are not killed they are maimed and crippled for life?"

She drew in her breath before she continued:

"And in the darkness there are not only explosions and underground fires and water in which children of five stand for hours every day, but there is no proper ventilation."

Her eyes met the Marquis's and she realised that he was looking at her with surprise.

The words tumbled from her lips as she continued:

"All the other mines in South Yorkshire have installed the Buddle Air-Pump that was invented nine years ago, but in the Havingham mine they cannot afford such luxuries!"

Her voice was bitter as she went on:

"Lord Fitzwilliam's mines use safety-lamps, but the Havingham mine cannot afford that either, nor can it afford any of the customary gifts or output bonuses."

As if she could not bear to look at him Torilla stood staring across the Park and said in a different tone:

"How do you think I feel when I hear how many race-horses you possess? That you are one of the richest men in England and that you have more possessions and more houses than you can count?"

The Marquis did not reply and she went on:

"Have you ever stopped to think how you could exist on a weekly wage of thirteen shillings and sixpence, which is all your miners get? Or how would you fare if you found that out of the three pounds ninepence you received a month eleven shillings and twopence had to be spent on candles and powder?"

Torilla's voice trembled as she added:

"But it is the children who haunt me; children who never have enough to eat; children who if they are frightened or sleepy in the stuffy darkness get beaten!"

There were tears now in her eyes, and because she had no wish for the Marquis to see them she turned her back on him to add:

"I knew before I came south that you were the Devil himself; a monster whom I ... cursed every day that I lived in Barrowfield. Do you really think I would want Beryl ... whom I love ... to marry ... y-you?"

The last words were almost incoherent.

As if she could bear it no longer, Torilla walked away, leaving the Marquis sitting behind her on the fallen tree.

She did not look back. It was in fact impossible to look anywhere, for her eyes were blinded by tears.

Only as she neared the Hall did she wipe them away fiercely with her handkerchief and on entering the house hurried up to her bed-room to wash her face and remove all traces, she hoped, of the emotions which had upset her.

"Now he knows the truth," she told herself defiantly, "and he will hate me as I hate him!"

Only as her agitation and her emotions subsided a little did she wonder what the Marquis had felt on hearing what she had revealed to him.

She remembered the surprise she had seen on his face, which seemed to be genuine, and she told herself that perhaps he really had no idea of the conditions in the Havingham mine.

But, still intent on hating him, she thought that was no real excuse for the conditions that existed there.

He owned the pit, the profit it made was his, and no man should exploit human beings without concerning himself with the conditions under which they laboured.

Even as she told herself this, she realised she was only repeating what her father had said.

Yet it was beyond doubt so true that she could find no extenuating excuses for the Marquis even if he had not been aware of what was happening in a pit which actually bore his name.

"I hate him!" she told herself as she went downstairs to breakfast with Beryl, to find to her relief that the Marquis was not present.

'I hate him!' she thought at luncheon.

There was a large number of guests but she found it impossible not to glance occasionally at the Marquis sitting at the other side of the table.

He had Beryl fawning on him on one side, and a very attractive married Peeress on the other.

'They do not care what he does,' Torilla thought scathingly.

Then remembering what she had felt when he touched her wrist, she thought that perhaps he had the same magical effect on other women.

"He has the charm and the guile of the Devil," she told herself severely. "He is everything that is wrong, wicked, and contemptible! But once he is married to Beryl, I shall seldom see him again."

Wondering why the thought was disspiriting rather than elating, she continued to force herself into remembering the conditions in Barrowfield and not to let them fade from her mind in the comfort, beauty, and luxury of Fernleigh Hall.

It was difficult, however, when Beryl told her there was to be a large dinner-party that night to celebrate her engagement.

"I want you to look attractive, dearest," she said to Torilla, "so come to my bed-room and we will choose one of my prettiest gowns for you to wear."

Torilla longed to reply that as far as she was concerned there was nothing to celebrate.

But it was impossible to refuse Beryl as she pulled glamorous and expensive gowns from her wardrobe, holding them up against Torilla to see the effect before finally deciding upon the one she thought suited her best.

"You look like a bride in white," she said, "and it is what I should wear. But Gallen has given me some magnificent turquoises and I have a gown of exactly the same colour."

"I could wear pink," Torilla suggested.

"Wear white and you will look like an angel," Beryl answered, "or should I say a saint?"

She gave a little laugh.

"Saint Torilla—that is what I think I will call you in the future. You are so good, my dearest, that you make me feel guilty when I think of all the things I have done of which you would disapprove."

"I am no saint," Torilla retorted in a low voice. "I also do things which I . . . know are . . . wrong."

"I do not believe it," Beryl expostulated. "You are good—you always have been. What is more, Torilla, you have the power of making other people want to be good."

"Please . . . please, Beryl . . . do not talk like that," Torilla said in a strange voice.

It made her feel inexpressibly guilty to know that she had allowed the Marquis to kiss her and was deceiving her cousin by not telling her.

But she had remembered her mother saying once many years ago:

"We should confess our sins to God, Torilla, but never, if it would hurt them, to other people."

Torilla had not understood exactly what her mother meant at the time, but now she knew there would be no point in making Beryl unhappy.

If anyone must bear the consequences of a wrong action, it should be the person who had done it.

"Whatever you may say, Torilla," Beryl went on, "you make me want to be good, and who knows—perhaps one day I shall succeed!"

She spoke seriously, then with a puckish look in her eyes she added:

"What a bore I should be! I am quite certain Gallen would leave me at once!"

She danced across the room, holding in her arms the white gown which she wished Torilla to wear.

"Can you not see how dull it would be for everyone if I became saintly and thought only of good works?" she teased. "Lord Newall would stop wishing to kiss me! Gallen would undoubtedly return to the arms of one of his flirts, and half the dressmakers and caterers in London would go out of business!"

She flung the white gown over a chair.

"No, no!" she laughed. "Each to his proper place: yours on a pedestal, mine in a bath of champagne!"

Torilla could not help laughing.

"A bath of champagne?" she questioned.

"It is really true that some of the beauties in London do bathe in champagne, because they think it is good for their skin," Beryl explained.

"I have never imagined such a thing!" Torilla said. "I know the Dandies use it for polishing their Hessians, but a whole bath of it . . . I have never heard of such ridiculous extravagance."

"People will do anything to look beautiful," Beryl said, "but thank goodness I do not have to trouble about my skin."

"It has always been quite perfect!" Torilla agreed.

"Like yours," Beryl replied. "Oh, I forgot to tell you . . ."

She turned from the mirror where she had been looking at her reflection to say impressively:

"Gallen likes you! I never expected he would. As I told you, he never speaks to girls."

Torilla longed to retort that whatever the Marquis felt about her it was of no importance, and she hated him.

Instead she found herself listening attentively, as if fascinated, to what Beryl had to impart.

"I asked him what he thought of my cousin and my greatest friend," Beryl related, "and do you know what he replied?"

"What . . . did he say?" Torilla asked.

"He said: 'She is a very unusual person, and exceptionally lovely'!"

Torilla found herself blushing.

"I am sure he was only being . . . polite," she said a little incoherently.

"You do not know Gallen if you think he would lie about that sort of thing," Beryl said. "He is usually brutally frank about people. He was the person who first said that Lady Jersey looked 'like an inquisitive parakeet!' and that Beau Brummel was a 'clothes horse on legs.'"

Beryl laughed.

"I assure you, Torilla, he administers more set-downs than he pays compliments. But I want him to like you, because once we are married you can come and stay with us and I will find you a suitable husband."

Torilla thought privately that it was very unlikely after what she had said to him today that the Marquis would welcome her to any house that he owned, but aloud she said:

"You are very kind to me, Beryl dearest, and thank you for the gown."

"I have told my maid to take a whole lot of things to your room already," Beryl said, "and they are packing them in readiness for our trip to London tomorrow."

"Thank you so very much," Torilla said again.

"There is also a whole heap of clothes in Curzon Street that I shall never wear again," Beryl added, "so you need not keep those rubbishy dresses you brought from the north. Tell the maids to put them on the bonfire."

"I will take them back with me," Torilla said firmly.

She knew that once she returned to Barrowfield she would feel over-dressed and far too ostentatious in anything Beryl might give her.

When she went downstairs to dinner and entered the Salon where already some people had arrived, she could not help looking at the Marquis to see if he noticed her.

It was wrong, she knew, to value in any way his opinion, yet because he had said she was beautiful when she was wearing the threadbare blue gown that Abby had made her, it was impossible not to wonder what he would think of her now!

She knew that the exquisite white gauze gown, which must have cost an astronomical sum, made her look sylph-like and showed off her figure to perfection.

Her fair hair had been dressed in a fashionable manner by one of the maids, and because she had no jewellery she had added a tiny spray of spring flowers.

She would not have been honest with herself if she had not realised when she looked in the mirror that she was very different from the dowdy girl who had dined with the Marquis at the George and Dragon.

What she did not realise was that, however fashionable the gown she was wearing, there was in her face and eyes a spirituality which made her appear different and somehow apart from the other people in the room.

Because she was so slim and so graceful she seemed almost to float rather than walk across the Salon. Then as her eyes met the Marquis's Torilla felt her heart behave in a very strange manner.

Quickly she looked away from him.

He did not speak to her or come near her all the evening, but seemed intent on making himself very pleasant to the guests who toasted his and Beryl's health.

They all proclaimed in fulsome tones the virtues of the engaged couple over and over again to anyone who would listen.

"It could not be a more suitable marriage," Lady Clarke said to Torilla.

"Yes . . . indeed, Ma'am," Torilla agreed.

"And it must be your turn next," Lady Clarke went on. She had known Torilla's family when they lived in Hertfordshire.

She put her hand on Torilla's shoulder as she said:

"I am sure you will find there are plenty of young men anxious to marry you who will not be put off by the fact that you are from a Vicarage and have no dowry."

She was an elderly woman and meant to be kind, but she made Torilla feel her own lack of importance.

Despite the fact that she had known many of the guests in the past, Torilla was glad when the evening was over.

They had departed, still expressing their delight at the engagement, and promising that all sorts of expensive presents would be delivered to the Hall in the near future.

"They are a lot of old hypocrites!" Beryl said when the last one left. "If I was not marrying Gallen I doubt if I should get anything better than a silver toast-rack!"

"They are all very fond of you, dearest," Torilla said.

"Nonsense!" Beryl retorted. "They have never ceased expressing their disapproval of me ever since I grew up. It is only now that I am on the way to becoming eminently respectable that they have found that they always admired my outrageous behaviour!"

Torilla thought that one of the most endearing things about Beryl was that she could laugh at herself.

"Well, thank goodness that is over!" the Earl said, coming into the Salon, "and when you get to London, Beryl, make it clear to your mother that I have no intention of putting up with any more junketing until the actual day of the wedding."

"I am sure Mama will be very disappointed if you refuse to escort us to the parties that are being given in my honour," Beryl replied.

"I will turn up in time to shake hands with all the fools who have nothing better to do than stuff themselves into St. George's, Hanover Square, to see you married—otherwise I am staying here with my horses and my dogs."

"I think that makes a lot of sense, Papa," Beryl said. "You know how unhappy you are among the *Beau Ton*."

She kissed her father and said:

"Tell Gallen when he comes in that I have gone to bed."

"Where is the Marquis?" Torilla asked curiously.

"I expect he is walking in the garden, feeling romantic all by himself," Beryl replied, "but I have no intention of joining him—I am far too tired."

She linked her arm through Torilla's.

"It is going to be amusing when we get to London," she said. "Gallen told me tonight that he is not joining us for a few days, so you will be able to meet Lord Newall. I am longing to hear what you think about him."

"Oh, Beryl, is that wise?" Torilla asked.

"It may not be wise, but it is a lot of fun!" Beryl replied. "And do not try to stop me, Saint Torilla. Every woman is entitled to a last fling before her wedding-day."

She kissed her cousin and whisked into her own bed-room before Torilla could reply.

Torilla lay awake for a long time thinking over the day and remembering with a sense of embarrassment the things she had said to the Marquis.

Could he be thinking over what she had told him, she wondered, while he walked round the garden alone?

She now wished that, once having started to speak of the pit, she had talked to him quietly and earnestly, explaining the horrors of what was happening rather than raging at him accusingly.

'Perhaps that was my chance to ask him to make a few reforms,' she thought, 'and I made a mess of it.'

She felt tears come into her eyes and gradually begin to run down her cheeks.

It all seemed such an inexpressible mix-up—the manner in which she had become involved with the Marquis, and the worry she felt about Beryl marrying without love.

And most of all, although she tried not to think of it, the wonder of his kiss, which she had treasured deep in her heart but which was now spoilt and besmirched because it had been . . . wrong.

*   *   *

London was, Torilla thought, even more fantastic than she had expected.

Her Aunt Louise had greeted them in characteristic style by telling Beryl sharply that she should have been there earlier, and hoping that Torilla intended to help rather than hinder her cousin.

It was just like the old days, Torilla thought, with her aunt breaking up their games because it was time for bed, or punishing them for quite inoffensive actions and ignoring completely those which were far more reprehensible.

The Countess of Fernleigh was different in every way from her younger sister Elizabeth.

Sometimes Torilla wondered if the reason she was often so sharp and even at times disagreeable was that she was not happy in her marriage as her sister had been.

It was painfully obvious that the Earl and Countess did not get on together, and they were, both of them, content to live most of the year apart.

The Countess, who was still extremely good-looking, had a large number of admirers who were always ready to squire her in her husband's absence.

As the Earl was completely content, as he put it, with his horses and dogs, they both lived the lives they wanted, which did not include each other's company.

'Perhaps all women need the protection of a husband,' Torilla thought, and it was obvious that the Countess thought in many ways she was misused.

"I suppose your father, as usual, is going to do nothing about the wedding, and leave everything to me," she said sharply soon after Beryl and Torilla arrived at Fernleigh House in Curzon Street.

"You know what Papa is like, Mama," Beryl replied.

"I do indeed," the Countess said acidly, "and I only hope he is prepared to meet the bills without making too much fuss about them."

"I am sure he will do that," Beryl replied carelessly, "especially if we do not ask him to do anything else except to write his name on the cheques."

"As long as he does that, I suppose I must accept the inevitable," the Countess remarked. "The first thing we must do tomorrow is choose your gown and, I suppose, Torilla's."

"It is very kind of you, Aunt Louise," Torilla said humbly.

"I cannot think why Beryl wants you to be her only bridesmaid," the Countess said in the tone of one who is determined to find fault. "I should have thought a retinue of at least ten would have been very effective."

"I wish on my wedding-day to be alone in my glory," Beryl said positively, "with, of course, the exception of Torilla. She can hold my bouquet, while a lot of gawky girls clumped behind me would spoil the whole effect."

"I see your point," the Countess said reflectively. "Is the Marquis sending the flowers for the Church from the Castle?"

"I have not the slightest idea," Beryl answered. "I leave those details to you, Mama."

"As I might have expected—I have to organise everything," the Countess said. "What you would do without me I cannot think."

Beryl threw out her hands.

"If you want me to say there would be a complete muddle, all right, Mama, I have said it!"

"You wait until you have to do everything yourself," the Countess said warningly, "you will then appreciate my difficulties for a change."

"You love every moment of it, Mama!" Beryl retorted. "You knew quite well that if Torilla or I tried to interfere we should soon be put outside the front door."

She laughed and added:

"Arrange everything your own way and do not forget you have to twist the Prince Regent round your little finger."

"I can do that when it comes to ceremonial occasions," the Countess said smugly. "His Royal Highness always says he likes my quite professional powers of organisation—which is more than can be said for that fatuous Lady Hertford."

"He loves her, Mama."

"God knows why," the Countess muttered.

She flounced out of the room and Beryl laughed as she said to Torilla:

"Poor Mama! She set her cap at the Prince Regent at one time, but she was a little too young for him, and much too thin. He likes fat, maternal, elderly women, and Mama did not qualify!"

When she saw the Prince Regent and met him the following night, Torilla could not imagine at first why anyone was interested in him as a man.

But she found when he talked to her that he had an aura of irresistible charm that made one forget that he was enormously fat, almost gross-looking, that his face was heavily powdered, and his stays creaked when he sat down.

"You are very pretty, my child," he said to Torilla, "and like your cousin you will soon have the *Beaux* buzzing round you like bees round a honey-pot."

"I am afraid I can never compete with Beryl, Sire," Torilla smiled.

"A very captivating young woman who has proved it by capturing the most captivating bachelor in captivity," the Prince said.

He liked the play on words and Torilla heard him repeating the sentence several times during the evening.

Everyone was asking where the Marquis was, in fact his name seemed to be on everybody's lips, and more than once Torilla heard in the crush at Carlton House remarks which made her apprehensive.

"The 'Incomparable' does not know what she is taking on where Gallen is concerned!" one *Beau* with his back to Torilla announced.

"Gallen would need a regiment of 'Incomparables' to keep him in order," a woman replied.

There was loud laughter before someone said:

"Can you imagine Havingham shackled in Holy Matrimony? Though I imagine it will not be in the least holy!"

"Not if he has anything to do with it," someone else quipped.

Torilla moved out of hearing.

It hurt her to hear such things and she told herself that she was concerned only for Beryl.

She could not help remembering how the Marquis had saved her from the odious attentions of Sir Joscelyn, or how kind he had been in looking after her until the last few minutes of their dinner together.

Even then he had done nothing to hurt or shock her.

She would not have been honest if she did not admit that she had been a willing accomplice to his sin, if that is what their kiss had been.

She had the inescapable feeling that had she struggled or shown that she wished to be free of him, he would have let her go.

Instead she had surrendered herself completely and utterly to his lips, and to the ecstasy which she knew she would be unable to forget even if she married a thousand times.

When it was time to leave Carlton House the Countess said:

"There is no sign of Beryl."

"I will find her, Aunt Louise," Torilla offered.

"She knew we arranged to leave at two o'clock," the Countess complained irritably. "It is just like Beryl to disappear when she is wanted. Look in the garden, Torilla; she is doubtless with some ardent swain and has forgotten the time."

With a little difficulty, because Carlton House was large and complex to anyone who had never been there before, Torilla found her way through an open window onto the terrace which overlooked the garden.

She stood against the stone balustrade, searching in the shadows under the trees that were lit with Chinese lanterns for Beryl's turquoise-blue gown.

It was impossible to distinguish her among the many women perambulating about on the arm of some splendidly decorated gentleman or glimpsed under the boughs of the trees.

'I shall have to go and look for her,' Torilla thought.

She walked along the terrace and found a flight of stone steps leading into the garden.

She went down them, looking to right and left, but there was no sign of her cousin.

Then when she was just about to turn back, thinking that perhaps Beryl would be at her mother's side by this time, she found what she sought.

At the very farthest end of the garden on the other side of a twisting, artificial stream arranged with fairy-lights there was a patch of turquoise.

Torilla could not see very clearly, but there was no doubt it was Beryl and she was clasped passionately in the arms of a tall man.

Torilla stood indecisive, wondering what to do.

It was quite impossible to think of interrupting them; at the same time, the Countess was waiting.

She stood looking at Beryl and now that her eyes were more accustomed to the darkness she could see that because the man who was kissing her was so tall her cousin was standing on tip-toe.

Torilla had never before seen two people kissing each other passionately in an embrace which vaguely she realised had been symbolic of love between a man and a woman all down the ages.

There was a strange, emotional beauty about it, and the mere fact that they were so close and oblivious of everything except themselves made her feel a little strange.

It was what she had felt, she thought, when the Marquis had kissed her.

She could not help wondering if Beryl was feeling as she had done, as if she were being lifted off the ground out of the world into a place that was part of the Divine.

The man holding Beryl so closely raised his head and now Torilla heard him say hoarsely:

"I love you! God in Heaven—how I love you! I cannot live without you!"

"I am afraid you will have to," Beryl answered, "for I intend to marry Gallen."

"How can you be so cruel? How can you torture me in such a manner? I swear I will kill myself!"

"And what good would that do?" Beryl enquired. "I shall not be able to join you in Hell, if that is where suicides go, for at least another forty or fifty years."

"Oh, Beryl! Beryl!" the man cried.

"Why do we not enjoy the world while we are both in it?" Beryl asked softly.

She raised herself once again on tip-toe and kissed him on the mouth.

"I will see you tomorrow at the Duchess of Richmond's. I must go now or Mama will be furious!"

"Stay. Do not leave me. I cannot bear it!"

He put out his arms to stop Beryl, but she was already moving away from him.

"Until tomorrow night, Charles!"

The man she had left groaned but made no attempt to follow her and Beryl moved to the right to cross the stream by a small bridge which Torilla had hitherto not noticed.

It was only then that she moved forward, saying:

"Beryl, there you are! Aunt Louise told me to come and look for you. It is time to leave."

"I thought Mama would be fussing," Beryl answered. "Have you enjoyed yourself?"

"Tremendously!" Torilla replied. "I hope you did."

They walked nearer the lights of the house, and now Torilla looked at her cousin, wondering if she would show any of the emotions on her beautiful face through which she must have passed.

Beryl looked exactly as usual except that there was a smile on her lips which somehow looked as if they had been kissed.

"Actually," Beryl said, "there were only a few moments when I did not find the whole evening a dead bore!"

Chapter Five

The Ball at Lady Melchester's was even more fantastic and extravagant than the other parties at which Torilla had been present since she arrived in London.

The Countess had, however, protested against Beryl and Torilla attending it.

"I cannot bear that Melchester woman!" she said disparagingly. "She is fast and her love-affairs are a scandal. I cannot imagine why you should wish to accept her over-pressing invitations."

"She gives good parties, Mama, and all my friends will be there," Beryl replied.

"She has nothing but money to recommend her," the Countess snapped, "but of course, I know that most of your friends care for little else."

Beryl laughed good-humouredly.

"That is because it is something that most of them lack," she replied.

She gave a little self-satisfied sigh.

"One comforting thought is that no-one can say that about Gallen."

"No, indeed," the Countess agreed, her voice softening, "and I am sure, Beryl, if you play your cards right he will prove a very generous husband."

"I will make sure of that," Beryl replied.

Torilla put down the book she was reading, and

rising from the sofa in the Drawing-Room she walked to the window.

She found it not only embarrassing but hurtful to listen to Beryl and her mother talking in such a manner about the Marquis.

She herself had thought many hard things about him, but it was different in the case of Beryl, who had no grounds for criticising him, or the Countess, who was quite obviously jubilant at the idea of such an advantageous marriage.

It suddenly struck her that the reason why he looked cynical was that the women he knew talked in such a hard and calculating manner and he was well aware of it.

Where she was concerned he was more perceptive and more intuitive than she had imagined any man could be. If he knew what she was thinking, surely he must be well aware also of Beryl's thoughts?

More and more as she saw them together she found herself praying that if her cousin was to marry the Marquis as she intended she would grow to love him.

"How can Beryl contemplate," Torilla asked herself, "the sort of marriage that exists between her father and mother?"

The Countess never missed an opportunity of criticising the Earl, and a day never passed without her saying something cutting and unkind which revealed all too clearly her feelings towards him.

Torilla wondered if Beryl would become the same sort of woman and she had a feeling she would.

Marriage, however rich the bridegroom might be, however luxurious their surroundings, could be nothing but a farce if the two people concerned in it did not love each other.

She could remember the tenderness in her mother's voice when she spoke to her father and could recall the look of adoration in the Vicar's eyes when her mother rose to kiss him every time he returned home.

Torilla could not imagine Beryl worrying over the Marquis, seeking in every way to make him happy, and sacrificing her own desires and interests for his.

Because she loved Beryl very deeply and sincerely, Torilla found herself growing more and more unhappy as their first week in London passed.

She was well aware that Beryl met Lord Newall at every party, and they always disappeared into the garden or to some part of the house where they would be alone.

Beryl had introduced him to her and Torilla found that Lord Newall was a good-looking man with dark, passionate eyes which seldom left Beryl's face.

There was an intensity about him that she could understand Beryl finding attractive, and yet because she knew her cousin so well she was well aware that while Beryl was amused by Lord Newall she was not really in love with him.

"Would you like to marry His Lordship?" Torilla had asked her one evening when they returned home after Beryl had disappeared for longer than usual in the garden of Bedford House.

"I am sure Charles would be a very ardent lover," Beryl replied, "but he has no money, and there is an old adage that says: 'When poverty comes in the door love flies out the window.' "

"Does money matter so very much when one is in love?" Torilla asked in a low voice.

"Of course it does!" Beryl answered.

Then after a moment's pause she said in a different tone:

"If one was really, completely, overwhelmingly in love I suppose one would forget everything else."

"That is what we used to say we both wanted," Torilla said softly.

"When we were young and knew nothing about men, we were absurdly romantic," Beryl retorted.

She sat down at her dressing-table as she spoke, and as if she deliberately changed the subject she said:

"I think I shall ask Gallen to give me sapphires as a wedding-present. Sapphires are very becoming to fair-haired women."

"We were talking about Lord Newall," Torilla said.

"I know," Beryl answered, "but we have really exhausted everything there is to say about him. His kisses are entrancing, but he has little else to recommend him."

Torilla gave a little cry.

"Do not talk like that, Beryl," she begged. "It is hard and horrid, and so unlike you used to be."

"Sometimes I feel hard and horrid," Beryl answered, "and I feel that life has paid me a shabby trick."

Torilla was surprised.

"How . . . what do you mean?"

"I'm talking nonsense," Beryl replied quickly, "I am tired. Go to bed, Torilla. There is another party to-morrow night and the night after that, and I want you to look your best."

Torilla knew their conversation was over, but when she went to her own room she lay for a long time thinking about Beryl and praying for her.

At the Melchester Ball she certainly did not look as if life had brought her anything but gaiety and beauty which made her outshine every other woman present.

With her gown embroidered with diamanté, with real diamonds round her neck and in her hair, Beryl glittered like a fairy on top of a Christmas-tree.

She was besieged by men wishing to dance with her, while Lord Newall looking dark and Byronic glowered ferociously.

It was quite obvious that Beryl was enjoying herself and Torilla found that she too was having a success.

In another of the beautiful gowns that Beryl had given her she did not feel insignificant among the elegant ladies glittering with jewels and eyeing each other with feline spitefulness.

Just occasionally Torilla found herself thinking that just a few of the diamonds they wore round their long necks or which hung from their ears like small chandeliers would keep a dozen miners' families in comfort for at least a year.

Then she remembered Abby's admonitions and forced herself to forget Barrowfield and to listen to the charming things that were being said to her by every man with whom she danced.

It was very hot in the Ball-Room and Torilla allowed herself to be persuaded to seek the coolness of the air in the large garden which surrounded the whole house.

If the Prince had made the gardens of Carlton House into a romantic bower, Lady Melchester had tried to out-vie him.

There were not only artificial streams with lights turning the water to different colours, there was a fountain which sprayed perfume instead of water and which was illuminated to look like a spray of liquid gold.

There was artificial fruit hanging from some of the trees, which when picked proved to be packets of bonbons or small amusing trinkets.

"It is all very imaginative," Torilla said to her partner.

"And all very expensive," he laughed. "Let us hope His Royal Highness being out-rivalled does not try to surpass such originality. He might decide to give all his guests expensive pictures or pieces of classical sculpture."

"It would be a lovely idea," Torilla laughed.

"Until the bills came in ... which of course would never be paid."

They both laughed again, then as they reached a seat that was unoccupied the gentleman with whom she had been dancing said:

"Shall I get you a glass of champagne? I must admit to feeling very thirsty."

"A glass of lemonade would be delightful," Torilla replied, "and I will wait here until you return."

"That is a promise," her partner said. "Do not let anyone steal you away or I shall be obliged to threaten him with pistols at dawn!"

Torilla laughed as he hurried away.

He was rather an amusing man whom she had danced with at various parties, and although he paid her plenty of compliments he did not actually make love to her, which she found a relief.

She was surprised to find that quite a number of men professed themselves to be in love with her, and one or two she thought were actually sincere.

For some reason, however, the moment their compliments became anything more than a polished and conventional exchange of words she found herself shrinking inside and making every effort later to avoid them.

She supposed it was shyness, and yet at the same time she was aware that what she shrank from was love, although she knew that Beryl would laugh at her for being foolish.

Several of the men who proposed marriage were, she imagined, extremely eligible, and she should in fact have been very grateful that they should even consider her as a wife.

But she knew, almost as soon as a certain look appeared in their eyes, that she could never in any circumstances consider them as a husband.

She did not know why she was so certain, but the conviction was there and there was nothing she could do about it.

"I thought Lord Arkley seemed very attentive to

you tonight," the Countess had said the previous evening as they were driving home.

Torilla looked embarrassed, but the Countess had gone on:

"He may be a little old for you, but it would be a good marriage. He was married when he was very young, but his wife died two years later, and there were no children."

She considered for a moment, then she said:

"Yes, I think Arkley would do you well. I shall ask him to dinner before the Dorchesters' Ball and try to find out if his intentions are serious."

"No ... please, Aunt Louise, please ... please do nothing of the sort," Torilla begged. "Even if ... Lord Arkley asked me to ... marry him I would not ... accept him."

"Would not accept him?" the Countess repeated, her voice rising. "What on earth do you mean by that, Torilla?"

"He is very ... pleasant," Torilla said hesitatingly, "but I ... know I could never ... love him."

"Love!" the Countess said sharply. "The sooner you get rid of such ridiculous, romantic notions, the better!"

"Torilla is an idealist, Mama," Beryl interposed. "She has always sworn that she will never marry a man unless she loves him. I think you are wasting your time in trying to persuade her into considering Lord Arkley."

"Torilla should realise," the Countess said sharply, "that it is the duty of every young girl to make a good marriage by the time she is nineteen, and Torilla is nearly that already."

"I would not wish ..." Torilla began.

"In your circumstances," her aunt interrupted, "without money and with little to recommend you except your looks, you must be grateful if you find a husband who will care for you and keep you in comfort."

Beryl laughed.

"I seem to have heard you, Mama, giving me this sort of lecture when I first came out."

"Fortunately, you were intelligent enough to realise that I was talking good common sense," her mother replied. "There were times this last year when I thought you were throwing away your chances, but I admit I was wrong. You waited, then Gallen came along, and what mother could ask for a better marriage for her daughter?"

There was an almost ecstatic note in the Countess's voice. Then she said in a different tone:

"Where you are concerned, Torilla, it is quite different. You cannot afford to wait, and the sooner you bring Lord Arkley up to scratch the better!"

"Aunt Louise . . ." Torilla began, only to receive a sharp kick from Beryl under the carriage-rug, which made the words die on her lips.

"It is no use arguing with Mama," Beryl said when they had reached Curzon Street and gone up to bed together. "Whatever you say to the contrary, she will only think you half-witted."

"I do not wish her to speak to Lord Arkley, as I am sure she intends to do," Torilla said in a frightened voice.

"Listen, dearest," Beryl said, "it does not have to be Lord Arkley, if you dislike him. But you know as well as I do that this is a big opportunity for you to find a husband."

She added almost sternly:

"Do you really want to go back to the north and meet no-one and see nobody of any importance? It cannot be very amusing in Barrowfield or whatever it is called."

She saw the expression on Torilla's face and put her arms round her.

"I love you, Torilla," she said. "I want you to be married, then we can both have fun together. I have really missed you these last two years."

"And I have missed you," Torilla said.

"Then marry somebody quickly," Beryl admonished, "so that we can move in the same Social World. Arkley is not a bad catch, and other men like him, which is important."

She was smiling and her eyes were twinkling as she added:

"And far safer than if it is women, which is my problem!"

Torilla laughed, she could not help it.

Beryl kissed her cheek.

"Think about it, Torilla, and be sensible. I know if Aunt Elizabeth were alive she would want you to have a home of your own."

Beryl's words echoed in Torilla's mind when she went to bed and she found herself talking to her mother as she so often did.

"I know you would want me to get married, Mama," she said in the darkness, "but not to someone I did not love . . . but perhaps I shall never love anyone as you loved Papa."

Almost insidiously the thought came to her that what she was looking for was in fact the feeling she had had when the Marquis kissed her.

It was because she knew she would never feel that rapture with Lord Arkley that she could not marry him.

It was because she had known that the other men who had begun to be passionate in their protestations could never give her that divine ecstasy she had felt with the Marquis that she had run away from them.

As if she was frightened of where her thoughts were leading her she buried her face in the pillow and tried to go to sleep.

* * *

Sitting in the garden at Lady Melchester's house, hearing the soft strains of music in the distance and the tinkle of the water as it cascaded down a small artificial waterfall, Torilla found herself thinking how conducive it all was to romance.

She was quite certain that somewhere in the garden Beryl was being made love to, if not by Lord Newall then by one of her other numerous admirers.

She thought perhaps there was something wrong with her because she was content just to look at the beauty round her and would only feel frightened if her partner expressed himself in words of love.

Her thoughts were interrupted by the knowledge that a man had crossed the stream and was coming towards her.

"You have been very quick . . ." she started to say, thinking her partner had returned with the drinks.

Then she gave a terrified start as she realised that the man advancing towards her was Sir Joscelyn Threnton.

"I thought I was not mistaken in recognising you in the Ball-Room, Miss Clifford," he said with a smile on his lips.

He sat down beside Torilla on the seat, turning sideways so that he could look at her.

She looked away from him, feeling acutely embarrassed and at the same time outraged when she remembered his behaviour.

"You are certainly more elaborately gowned than when I last saw you," he said, and as the colour rose in her cheeks he laughed quietly.

"Please . . . leave me alone," Torilla said, finding her voice with some difficulty.

"That is something I have no intention of doing," Sir Joscelyn replied. "We were most unfortunately interrupted when we last met, but I have every intention of renewing our acquaintanceship."

"That, Sir, is something I will not permit. Will you please leave me?"

Torilla spoke firmly and now she was not so afraid.

The shock of seeing Sir Joscelyn had made her for a moment too confused to think clearly, but now she told herself there was nothing he could do to hurt her.

There were a large number of people within ear-shot and her partner would be returning at any moment.

"I have a marked aversion to being pipped at the post," Sir Joscelyn said, "although of course I had no idea when I came to your room at the Peligan that you were under the protection of the Marquis of Havingham."

Torilla turned to stare at him in astonishment.

"What . . . are you . . . saying?"

Sir Joscelyn smiled, and there was something very unpleasant about it.

"Does Lady Beryl know that her cousin accompanied the Marquis unchaperoned on his journey south?"

"How dare you make such a suggestion!" Torilla said indignantly. "The Marquis overheard the disgraceful way in which you were behaving towards me, and as a complete stranger he came to my rescue. I had never met him and had no idea who he was."

"That is your story," Sir Joscelyn said. "I only hope that Lady Beryl believes it."

"Lady Beryl does not . . ."

Torilla stopped suddenly.

She realised too late that what she was about to say was exactly what Sir Joscelyn wanted to learn.

"So—you have not told your cousin," he said after a moment's silence. "That is what I suspected. Well, I imagine the information will be of interest to her. I must ask her for the next dance."

Torilla gave a little cry.

"No . . . please," she said. "Please do not . . . speak of . . . this to . . . Beryl."

Even as she spoke she knew by the expression on Sir Joscelyn's face how much he was enjoying having her, so to speak, in his power.

She had seen him humiliated when the Marquis turned him out of her bed-room, and she knew this

was his revenge: to hurt Beryl, as she could not bear
to think of her being hurt.

She thought wildly that if only she had told Beryl
the truth as soon as she arrived at Fernleigh Hall everything would have been all right.

But it was because Sir Joscelyn's behaviour was
irrevocably woven into the kiss that the Marquis had
given her the succeeding evening that she could not
bring herself to speak of it.

Now she felt as if the ground opened in front of
her and there was a bottomless gulf yawning at her
feet.

"I am prepared to bargain with you," Sir Joscelyn
said.

"Bargain?" Torilla asked sharply.

"You are asking me to keep silent on a matter
which I feel is of considerable interest to all the parties
concerned, but my silence has a price."

"I think that is called 'blackmail,'" Torilla said.

"Correct!" Sir Joscelyn agreed. "I intend to blackmail you, lovely Miss Clifford, because, as I have said,
I do not like losing a race when I am actually at the
winning-post."

"Your ... behaviour was ... despicable, as you
... well know," Torilla said in a low voice.

"It was entirely your fault for being so alluring,"
Sir Joscelyn replied lightly. "And now—do you want
to hear my terms?"

Torilla did not answer and after a moment he
said:

"They are quite simple. Either you dine with me
alone tomorrow evening, or pay me the sum of five
thousand pounds. The choice is yours!"

Torilla turned to look at him.

"D-dine with you ... alone?" she faltered.

"There is a little place off Jermyn Street where
they have private rooms. No-one will see you there
and we can renew our acquaintance where it was, unfortunately, broken off."

Torilla saw by the look in his eyes exactly what he intended and she made a little sound of sheer horror as she turned her face away from him again.

"On the other hand," Sir Joscelyn said, "my pride would be slightly mollified by the sum of five thousand pounds."

"How could I . . . possibly find a . . . sum like that?" Torilla asked.

"It would not seem very large to the gentleman who came to your rescue."

"The . . . Marquis?" Torilla breathed.

"Exactly—the Marquis!" Sir Joscelyn said. "He is always quite prepared to pay for his amusements, and I think you will find he agrees that I am really being very reasonable in this matter, considering that his engagement to the 'Incomparable' Lady Beryl was announced the following day."

There was something very menacing in the way Sir Joscelyn spoke, and at the same time it was almost as if he smacked his lips over the fact that he had such excellent cards to play.

Torilla sat astounded. She could not think of what to say or do and everything seemed to be twirling round in her head in a hopeless confusion.

"My Club is Boodles," Sir Joscelyn said. "If I do not receive a cheque for five thousand pounds there by noon tomorrow I shall expect you, Miss Clifford, at Duke's Hotel at seven o'clock."

He reached out as he spoke and took one of Torilla's hands from her lap.

"I can honestly say," he said in a low voice, "that I am hoping you do not have the courage to ask the Marquis to pay up."

Before he could kiss her hand Torilla snatched it from him. Then without waiting for him to leave her she ran across the garden towards the house.

She felt Sir Joscelyn was pursuing her, enveloping her, and she could not escape from him.

The Ball-Room was on the first floor and there

were steps leading from the garden to the balcony which ran the whole length of the house.

Hastily Torilla climbed them.

She wanted the safety and security of the crowd; she wanted to get away from Sir Joscelyn and the terror of what he had suggested to her.

Then as she reached the last step leading up to the balcony she saw a man standing alone looking out into the garden. Her heart turned over in her breast.

It was like finding a sudden haven of security in the middle of a tempestuous sea.

Without remembering anything that she had felt about him except that he had saved her before from Sir Joscelyn, Torilla ran towards the Marquis.

She reached his side and put out her hands, which were trembling, towards him.

"You are ... here! You are ... back!" she cried incoherently. "I need you ... I need your ... help!"

Her voice was tremulous in her desperation and as the Marquis turned to look down at her she saw that he raised his eye-brows.

"What has happened?" he asked.

She thought his calm, drawling voice was like a life-line thrown to a drowning man.

"I must ... speak to you ... I must ... talk to you ... alone."

"But of course," he answered. "Shall we go out into the garden?"

"No ... no!" Torilla said quickly, thinking they might encounter Sir Joscelyn.

"Then we will find somewhere else," the Marquis said.

He gave her his arm and she put her hand on it, feeling that she must hold on to him in case he escaped her.

She was experiencing again all that she had felt when Sir Joscelyn first assaulted her in the bed-room of the Peligan. Her heart was thumping in her breast, her lips were dry, and the constriction in her throat made it hard to speak.

The Marquis avoided the windows opening into the Ball-Room, which was crowded with dancers, and led Torilla to one at the far end of the house.

Here there was a small Sitting-Room arranged with sofas and shaded lights. It was, however, occupied by several couples, and the Marquis passed through it to walk across a landing and open a door which was marked "Private."

He seemed to know his way about and Torilla found they were in a part of the house that was not so brilliantly lit and appeared to be deserted except for themselves.

The Marquis led the way and they entered a room which Torilla saw was decorated in very feminine taste and redolent with the fragrance of flowers.

She had an idea later that it was the private *Boudoir* of their hostess, but for the moment she could think of nothing save that she was alone with the Marquis and could tell him what had happened.

He indicated a sofa and she sank down on it, her eyes very dark and frightened in her pale face.

Looking at her, the Marquis realised he had seen such an expression on her face once before.

"Tell me all about it," he suggested, and he was not drawling.

Torilla clasped her hands together, but as she opened her lips to speak she realised how embarrassing it would be to explain to the Marquis what Sir Joscelyn had insinuated about them.

Then she told herself that what she must primarily be concerned with was to prevent Beryl from being told such lies; for since she had never mentioned what had happened on the journey, Beryl might think there was some truth in Sir Joscelyn's story.

She raised her eyes to the Marquis's face and said in a very low voice:

"It is . . . Sir Joscelyn!"

The Marquis frowned.

"What has that swine done now?" he asked sharply.

"He . . . spoke to me just . . . now in the . . . garden," Torilla answered. "He said terrible . . . things and I do not . . . know what to do."

"What did he say?"

Torilla felt that the embarrassment of it made it almost impossible for her to speak.

The Marquis waited, and although she turned her face away and her voice was almost inaudible the words had to be spoken.

"H-he . . . threatened to t-tell . . . Beryl that we were . . . together at the Peligan!"

The Marquis swore beneath his breath.

"I might have guessed that was the sort of construction he would put on it," he said sharply.

"He . . . s-said that he was . . . prepared to m-make a b-bargain."

"What sort of bargain?"

Again it was hard to answer the question.

"He . . . s-said," Torilla faltered after a moment, "that I could either . . . dine . . . alone with him . . . t-tomorrow night in a . . . p-private room, or I m-must pay him . . . five thousand pounds before n-noon."

"So that is his game!" the Marquis said quietly.

He bent forward and put one hand over Torilla's fingers, which she had been entwining together in her agitation.

"It is all right, Torilla," he said. "I will deal with this. I know this type of bounder, and I promise you shall not be troubled any further."

"I am not w-worrying about . . . myself," Torilla said, "b-but . . . Beryl."

The Marquis's fingers on hers gave her the same feeling she had felt before when he touched her in the Park.

She felt a streak of lightning stab through her; she

had an irrepressible impulse to cling to his hand, to hold on to him tightly and beg him to take care of her.

It was not only Sir Joscelyn, she thought wildly, it was Lord Arkley, her aunt manoeuvring her into marriage, and what she herself felt about the men who approached her.

Then she told herself severely that the Marquis belonged to Beryl and things were complicated enough without her relying on him as she longed to do.

The Marquis sensed her agitation and said quietly:

"It is all right. I promise you it will be all right."

"If only I had ... told Beryl that we had met when I first ... arrived at the Hall," Torilla said.

"Why did you not do so?" the Marquis asked in his deep voice.

Torilla found it impossible to answer him.

How could she say that, while she knew she should be ashamed of behaving as she had with a stranger, it had been the most wonderful thing that had ever happened in her life?

As if he knew the conflict in her mind, and understood, the Marquis rose to his feet.

"Go back to the Ball-Room and enjoy yourself, Torilla. Leave me to deal with everything."

"Supposing ... Sir Joscelyn ... ?"

"He will do nothing to hurt either you or Beryl," the Marquis answered. "I have asked you to trust me even though you think you cannot do so."

"I do ... trust you," Torilla answered.

"Despite the things you think about me?"

She raised her eyes to his face and now it was impossible to look away.

She felt that, without his touching her, she was captive in his arms, held by a spell that made her feel as if they reached out to each other across eternity.

Then abruptly, as if he forced himself to do so, the Marquis looked away from her and said in a different tone of voice:

"Your father sends you his love and hopes you are enjoying yourself."

"M-my . . . father?"

Torilla thought she could not have heard him correctly.

"I have been to Barrowfield," the Marquis explained. "I spent some time with your father and I think you will be glad to know that everything he suggested will be put into operation immediately."

"Do you . . . mean . . . ?" Torilla asked, and she could hardly breathe the word.

"The Buddle Air-Pump, the safety-lamps, new water-pumps, better safety precautions—there is a whole list of them!"

"I do not . . . understand," Torilla said, but there was a light in her eyes.

"You were right," the Marquis said, "completely and absolutely right in what you said to me. The pit is indeed a hell that should never have been allowed to exist."

Torilla could only stare at him, speechless, as he went on:

"I have sacked the Overseer and your father helped me to engage another man. I have forbidden the employment of children under the age of sixteen in my mine, and where it is possible women will be excluded altogether."

Torilla clasped her hands together.

"I think I am . . . dreaming."

"Your father said very much the same thing," the Marquis smiled. "There will be presents of money and pieces of beef at Festivals and for the old, and as in the Fitzwilliam mines there will be work incentives: four shillings for 'takking brass' when the men work a full week of six days, besides an increase in their ordinary wages."

Torilla gave a little cry.

"How could you do . . . anything so wonderful . . . so marvelous!"

"It is only what you told me to do."

"But I never thought . . . I never dreamt . . ."

She suddenly put her hands up to her face.

"I knew afterwards that I should have asked you to help, instead of attacking you as I . . . . did."

"I deserved it," the Marquis said. "I am the last person to plead ignorance when it is a case of neglect. I deserved everything you said to me, Torilla, and a great deal more."

"And now it will . . . all be . . . changed," she said, and there were tears in her eyes.

"A coal mine is always a coal mine, and not a pleasant place for anyone, especially someone like you," the Marquis answered. "But your father is satisfied."

"How can I ever thank you?"

Even as she spoke the colour rose in her face as she remembered that she had asked the same question once before.

The Marquis, she knew, thought the same thing, and once again her eyes were held by his.

"Now that that is settled," the Marquis said very quietly, "what are you going to do about us?"

Torilla was still.

"Us?" she whispered.

"Yes—us!" the Marquis repeated. "We both knew what happened when I kissed you, and yet I let you go because I believed I would never see you again and perhaps in time I could forget."

He drew in his breath.

"But we have met again, Torilla, and now I know I cannot live without you."

It was what she felt about him, Torilla thought wildly, and she knew it was the answer to everything that had perplexed and confused her.

Everything that she had been feeling, searching for, and worried about was because she had fallen in love when he touched her lips.

She had tried to fight against it, she had tried to

deny it, but it was love. The love her mother had felt for her father and he for her.

Love that was Divine, and yet very human, love that made it impossible for her to think of ever belonging to any other man.

"I love you, Torilla!"

The Marquis spoke the words very slowly and yet they seemed to vibrate through her.

"B-Beryl!"

She whispered the word, and yet it seemed to Torilla as she spoke that it was trumpeted round the room to echo and re-echo.

"Yes—Beryl," the Marquis answered.

He walked towards the mantelpiece to stand looking down into the fireplace, which was filled with flowers, as if he thought somehow among them he would find a solution.

Torilla stood looking at him, his broad shoulders, his athletic body, his dark head.

Now that the barriers were down, she knew that she loved him with her whole being, her mind, her body, and her soul. Everything she was was his.

"I will go to Beryl and tell her the truth," the Marquis said.

"No, you . . . cannot do . . . that."

"I will ask her to release me from a marriage which could only bring unhappiness to both of us."

"Beryl wants to . . . marry you," Torilla said, "and you know as well as I do that it would . . . hurt her socially in a . . . manner that would be . . . indefensibly cruel if you . . . jilted her."

"Perhaps I could persuade her to refuse me."

Torilla made a helpless little gesture with her hands.

"She would never do that. And you know also there could be no happiness for us if we . . . hurt Beryl and caused a scandal."

The Marquis turned to face her.

"You are saying all the things I expected you to

say," he said. "But how can we go on without each other?"

His face was suddenly drawn and there was an expression of pain in his eyes that made Torilla long to put her arms round him and comfort him.

She knew that what he was suggesting was wrong, completely wrong.

At the same time, she thought wonderingly that she had taken it for granted that he was asking her to marry him, although he had not actually said the words.

Once again he read her thoughts and said quietly:

"You know that I want more than my hope of Heaven to make you my wife, Torilla. I have laughed at love; I told my mother it was something that would never happen to me. But I have been confounded by my own words."

He paused before he went on:

"I love you as I did not think it possible to love any woman. Your face is always before my eyes. At night I hold you in my arms as I held you once, then, fool that I was, let you go."

"It was ... wrong of me to let you ... kiss me," Torilla whispered.

"It was not wrong but inevitable, something that was bound to happen, because without knowing it I have always been looking for you, and I think perhaps, my darling, you have been looking for me."

That was true, Torilla thought, but she had not been aware of it. Only now did she know that he was everything she had ever dreamt of ... imagined ... her ideal.

"Would you be brave enough to come away with me?" the Marquis asked. "To go abroad where we could be married and live quietly for a few years until the scandal and gossip died down? People forget very quickly."

"How could we ... do that to ... Beryl?" Torilla questioned.

At the same time, she thought that nothing could be more wonderful, more perfect, than to be with him and to have nothing to distract their minds from each other.

Then she told herself it would be wrong and wicked to take her happiness at the expense of someone she loved as she loved Beryl.

"I love you," she said softly, "I shall always ... love you and there could never be ... another man whom I could ... marry."

At her words the Marquis took a step towards her, a light in his eyes.

"But I cannot go ... away with you," Torilla finished. "We must ... forget that we have ever said such things to ... each other. You belong to Beryl. She has promised to become your wife and I would not allow you to do ... anything that was ... dishonourable."

Her voice trembled on the word and the Marquis with an inexpressible pain in his voice said:

"I might have known it would be a punishment for all my sins that I should fall in love with someone as good and pure as you."

"I am neither," Torilla said, "but we could not ... build our ... happiness on ... cruelty."

The Marquis sighed, and it seemed to Torilla almost a cry of pain.

"Perhaps we will find a solution," he said, but his voice was dull.

"There will not be one," Torilla answered despairingly, "but I shall pray for you and wherever you go ... whatever you do ... I shall pray that my love will keep you safe and ... perhaps in some ... little way ... inspire you."

"As you have inspired me already," the Marquis said. "Ever since you and I met, Torilla, I have found myself thinking in a manner in which I have never thought before, wanting to give instead of take."

He put his hand over his eyes as he said:

"When I saw the conditions in the pit which bears

my name, I was appalled, humiliated, and ashamed. I would not have felt like that if I had not known you."

"You would have had eyes to see what was wrong and you would have done something to improve it," Torilla said.

The Marquis looked at her, then he asked:

"You believe in me?"

"I believe in you, I trust you, and I think you are not only magnificent," Torilla replied, "but very . . . very . . . wonderful."

There was a little break in her voice and her eyes filled with tears as she looked at the Marquis.

"Then I will try not to fail you," he said.

It was in the nature of a vow.

As if they both knew their conversation had come to an end and there was nothing left to say, they moved towards the door.

The Marquis opened it for her and they went out.

Torilla felt as they walked away down the passage that they had left their hearts behind in that quiet, fragrant room.

Chapter Six

Beryl burst into the room where Torilla was writing a letter to her father.

"What do you think, Torilla?" she asked excitedly. "Gallen fought a duel this morning at dawn!"

As she spoke she walked across the room to the mirror so she did not see Torilla spring up from the desk, her face deathly pale, her lips moving though no sound came from them.

"You must admit it is really romantic," Beryl went on, regarding her reflection, "because of course he fought over me!"

"He is . . . not hurt?"

Torilla managed to say the words but they were hardly audible.

"Charles tells me that Gallen received a slight scratch, but his opponent is at death's door."

"Who . . . was it?"

Torilla could not help the question even though she knew the answer.

"A man called Sir Joscelyn Threnton," Beryl replied, taking off her bonnet and smoothing down her hair. "I believe I have met him, but I cannot remember what he looks like."

"And the Marquis is . . . not really h-hurt?"

"He should not actually have received a scratch,

129

so Charles says," Beryl answered, "but Sir Joscelyn fired before the referee had counted ten."

She gave a little laugh.

"It is so like Gallen's luck for him to sense what would happen and as Sir Joscelyn fired step to one side. Instead of killing him, the bullet merely grazed his left arm."

Beryl made a sound of delight as she went on:

"Charles says all the Clubs in St. James's are talking about it. Sir Joscelyn is completely discredited and if he recovers will have to go abroad."

Torilla clasped her hands together but she did not speak.

"If he stays," Beryl said with satisfaction, "no-one will speak to him and he will be ostracised."

Torilla felt her legs could no longer support her and she sat down on a chair.

How could she ever imagine . . . how could she have guessed that the Marquis would solve their problem in such a manner?

"You are quite . . . certain," she said, because she had to know, "that the Marquis is really not . . . badly wounded?"

Beryl threw herself down on the sofa.

"How you do fuss, Torilla!" she said. "Of course Gallen is all right. You must have realised by now that he is indestructible."

She leaned back against the satin cushions to add:

"I wonder what Sir Joscelyn said about me. Charles is certain he must have disparaged me in a most disgraceful manner for Gallen to call him out."

She sighed.

"I suppose I shall never know, for Gallen will certainly not tell me."

"Have you seen him?" Torilla asked.

"Who—Gallen?" Beryl asked. "I imagine he is at his house, and it would be most improper for me to call there without a chaperon!"

She was not speaking seriously but she added:

"Not a word of this to Mama! You know how she worries over anything that concerns my reputation, and it is not 'done' to be duelled over."

"I will not say anything," Torilla murmured.

At the same time, she felt like crying in her relief that the Marquis was not badly hurt.

Supposing Sir Joscelyn had succeeded in wounding him mortally? Suppose he had died?

She pushed the thoughts away from her mind. The Marquis was all right and she must not show herself to be a coward; but she knew she was one where he was concerned.

"I think everything has happened to me now," Beryl said. "Men have threatened before to fight over me, but it has never actually happened. This will certainly be something to relate to my grandchildren, if I ever have any."

She was speaking in her frivolous voice, which made Torilla wince.

She knew that if she were in Beryl's position at the moment she would be desperate with anxiety.

Whether it was conventional or not she would have been unable to prevent herself from going to the Marquis's side.

Beryl rose from the sofa.

"I only hope that this does not mean that Gallen will cry off taking us to the Opera tonight. It is to be a very smart occasion, and we are to be in the Prince Regent's box."

"We?" Torilla questioned.

"But of course—the invitation includes you, dearest," Beryl said. "The Prince said some very flattering things about you to Mama, and after the Opera is over we are all going to supper at Carlton House."

Torilla turned her head to look at the letter she had been writing to her father.

"I . . . suppose, Beryl," she said in a low voice, "you really . . . want me to stay with you for your

wedding? I feel I ought to . . . return to look after . . .
Papa."

Beryl gave a scream.

"Are you crazy? Of course you must stay for my
wedding! You are my bridesmaid, and I want you.
You know full well there would be no fun for me if
you are not here to laugh about everybody and see the
amusing side of it all."

With an effort Torilla said:

"I will . . . stay, if you really . . . want me, dearest.
It was . . . just a thought."

"And a very foolish one," Beryl said. "Now, that
you are back in my life again, I have no intention of
losing you, and if you raise more objections I shall
write to your father myself."

She smiled as she added:

"I shall point out to Uncle Augustus that Parsons
are supposed to be unselfish and if he takes you away
from me it will be very, very selfish indeed!"

This was Beryl's parting shot as she left the room.
Torilla put her hands up to her face.

She was still feeling rather faint from the shock of
thinking the Marquis had been injured, and it brought
home to her very forcefully how much she loved him.

She had lain awake all last night after they left
the Ball, feeling one moment a strange, unearthly happiness because he had said he loved her, and the next
moment feeling cast into the darkness of hell because
she knew they could never be together and that Beryl
stood between them like a flaming sword.

She could not believe that what she felt for the
Marquis and he for her was wrong or wicked. Love
could never be that.

What they were feeling was sacred, but Torilla
knew it would soil and defame what was divine if they
hurt Beryl and took their happiness at her expense.

She had been right when she told the Marquis she
would not let him do anything that was dishonourable.

She knew enough of the world to be aware that

however reprehensibly the Marquis might have behaved where his love-affairs were concerned, he had never done anything that broke the unwritten code expected of an honourable gentleman.

Just as he would never pull his horses on a racecourse, cheat at cards, or, like Sir Joscelyn, fire in a duel before the count of ten, so he could not refuse to marry Beryl, having once asked her to be his wife.

"I love him for what he is, and nothing must I ever do to spoil the man who is admired as a Corinthian and a sportsman," she said to herself.

When she thought of all he had done at Barrowfield because she had asked it of him, she thought that no man could have been more generous or openminded.

He had not made excuses for his neglect of the pit in the past, he had condemned his own ignorance and made what retribution he could.

He had said her father was satisfied, and she knew that in that case the changed conditions at his pit would surpass all the others in South Yorkshire.

The Marquis did not go to the Opera that night, on, Beryl was told, his doctor's orders, but Torilla fancied that there was perhaps another, more personal reason.

They both had to adjust themselves to what had been said in the privacy of the *Boudoir* at the Ball. It was going to be difficult to meet in public without revealing their feelings.

In the days that followed, Torilla saw the Marquis only when a large number of people were present and he made no attempt to speak to her alone.

Because they were so closely attuned to each other, she knew even when she looked at him across a crowded room that he was suffering.

He appeared to have grown thinner, the lines of cynicism on his face were sharply etched, but to Torilla they were lines of pain.

She learnt inadvertently from one of the grooms

that the Marquis was riding his horses to the point of exhaustion.

She herself found it almost impossible to eat the rich meals she had enjoyed when she first came south, and as the day of the wedding drew nearer Beryl asked her anxiously:

"What are you doing to yourself, Torilla? You are so thin that my gowns are beginning to hang on you like a sack! If you go on like this we will have to have your bridesmaid's gown altered."

"It fits very well," Torilla protested, and did not add that she had already had the waist taken in by two inches.

It was a very beautiful gown and she knew that she should be grateful to her aunt for giving it to her. But she felt almost as if it were a shroud that would cover her last glimpse of happiness.

She had already determined that when she went north after the wedding she would never return.

Because Beryl was his wife, it would be impossible to see the Marquis without feeling an irrepressible pang of jealousy, if not bitterness.

Every night Torilla prayed that she would feel neither of these things.

"I love them both," she said, "and I want them to be happy. Help me, God, to make my love overcome all other emotions. Help me! Help me!"

It was the cry of a frightened child, and she was afraid because it was impossible not to feel her whole body and mind yearning for the Marquis.

She longed for him so desperately that at times it threatened her self-control.

Beryl had herself designed Torilla's bridesmaid's gown: it was of white satin decorated round the hem with white roses which glittered with diamanté as if they were little drops of dew.

There were roses in a wreath which was very becoming on Torilla's fair hair and she was to carry a bouquet of the same flowers.

Beryl came to the last fitting.

"You look absolutely lovely, dearest!" she exclaimed, "and almost like a bride yourself."

"That's true, M'Lady," the dressmaker said. "I hope I shall be making a wedding-gown for Miss Clifford in the very near future."

"I think that is very likely," Beryl said with a smile, and Torilla knew she was thinking of Lord Arkley.

She wanted to repudiate such an idea, then she told herself there was no point in protesting and saying she had no intention of marrying Lord Arkley or any other man for that matter.

She knew Beryl would not understand, and she was quite certain her aunt when she had time was still intriguing on her behalf.

Fortunately, the Countess was so engrossed with the innumerable arrangements involved in Beryl's wedding that she had little time to worry about her niece.

But Torilla knew it was at the back of her mind, and she was determined as soon as the ceremony was over to return to Barrowfield, where it would be impossible for her aunt to concern herself with her.

"I do not think there is any more we can do to the gown," Beryl said.

"No, Your Ladyship. It's finished and I'll send it to Curzon Street tomorrow."

"Thank you," Beryl said, "and please send my gown as well."

"Very good, Your Ladyship."

"Do you realise I have not yet seen your wedding-dress?" Torilla said. "Do show it to me!"

Beryl shook her head.

"I am keeping it as a surprise. I have not allowed even Mama to look at it."

"I thought Aunt Louise must have seen it," Torilla said in surprise.

"No-one has seen it," Beryl answered, "have they, Madame?"

The dressmaker shook her head.

"It's going to be a very big surprise, M'Lady, not only for your family but all the other ladies who have been exceedingly curious as to what you'll be wearing."

Torilla looked rather apprehensively at her cousin. She knew Beryl well enough to guess that she was "up to something," and she could not help being curious as to what it might be.

The wedding was to be the last big event of the Season, because after it was over, the Prince Regent had announced, he was going to Brighton.

Already it appeared there would not be a seat to spare at St. George's, Hanover Square, and the Countess was growing more and more frantic as wedding-presents poured in to Curzon Street and to the Marquis's house in Park Lane.

They all had to be listed so that later they could be properly acknowledged.

"If anyone thinks I am going to spend my honeymoon writing letters of thanks for this collection, they are mistaken!" Beryl exclaimed.

She and Torilla were unpacking a dozen parcels which had been delivered that morning.

"Some of the things are nice," Torilla remarked.

"As far as I am concerned they are a lot of junk!" Beryl replied scathingly. "Look at this garnet brooch! Can you see me wearing garnets when Gallen has a collection of rubies worth a King's ransom?"

"It was sent to you by an old lady who knew us when we were children," Torilla said. "She says in her letter that it belonged to her great-grandmother and she has really made a great sacrifice in giving it to you."

"I do not want people to make sacrifices for me," Beryl replied sharply.

She got up from the floor where she had been sitting to open the parcels.

"Leave all this for the servants to clear up," she said, "I am tired of presents."

Torilla looked at her in surprise.

Beryl had been irritated and on edge for the past two days and had ceased to take any interest in the arrangements.

Torilla had a feeling that she was not happy.

"What is wrong, dearest?" she asked.

"Wrong? Why should there be anything wrong?" Beryl retorted.

Torilla told herself that she must be suffering from pre-wedding nerves, or perhaps she was getting a cold.

"Let us put on our bonnets and go out for a little while," Beryl suggested.

Torilla looked at the clock.

"It is after four. Aunt Louise should be home soon."

"Then that is all the more reason for getting away," Beryl said. "I am sick of hearing about the size of the congregation and wondering whether we should have more meringues and fewer cream-puffs at Carlton House."

Torilla did not reply and they went up the stairs in silence.

As they reached the landing outside Beryl's bed-room her maid appeared to say:

"Your wedding-gown has just been delivered, M'Lady, and I've put Miss Torilla's in her wardrobe."

"Thank you," Torilla said.

Beryl walked towards her bed-room door, then as she reached it she looked back at Torilla.

"Come and see my gown," she said. "I hope you admire it."

She opened the door and Torilla followed her.

She had expected from what had already been said that Beryl would wear something original, but the gown which lay on the big bed was certainly different from anything she had expected. It was pink!

A very pale pink, and it was in fact an exquisitely beautiful creation.

But who, Torilla asked herself in astonishment, had ever heard of a bride wearing pink?

The gown was of tulle and like Torilla's had roses round the hem. The train, which was very long, was encrusted with roses all glittering with diamanté dewdrops.

It was original, slightly theatrical, and at the same time Torilla knew that Beryl would look outstandingly beautiful.

The only question was—would the Marquis mind his bride being married in so unconventional a colour?

"I shall have a pink wreath on my head," Beryl said, "and as you see there is also a pink veil which will reach right to the ground."

She looked at her cousin almost defiantly as she spoke and after a moment Torilla answered:

"It is lovely, dearest, and you will look very beautiful, but you would have looked just as lovely in white."

There was a moment's pause. Then Beryl said in a hard, tight little voice:

"That is a colour I am not entitled to wear!"

Torilla looked at her in surprise, then her eyes widened.

"Beryl!" she exclaimed. "What ... are you ... saying?"

"I am telling you the truth."

Torilla drew in her breath.

"Do you mean ... are you really ... saying, Beryl ... that you ... ?"

"That I am not a pure, virgin bride?" Beryl finished. "That is exactly what I am telling you, Torilla. You might as well know the truth."

"B-but ... dearest," Torilla stammered. "It is ... Lord Newall you love? ... Then why ... ?"

"Charles Newall has nothing to do with it," Beryl replied. "The man to whom I gave myself was—my husband!"

Torilla stared at her as though she thought she had taken leave of her senses. Then with a little cry

Beryl sat down on the stool in front of her dressing-table and put her hands up to her eyes.

"Oh . . . Torilla . . . I wanted to tell you before . . . but what is the use? I have been so . . . desperately unhappy . . . but it does not . . . help to talk about it."

Torilla ran forward to kneel beside Beryl and put her arms round her.

"Tell me now," she pleaded. "Tell me, dearest."

The tears were running down Beryl's face.

"I loved him, Torilla. I loved him with . . . all my heart . . . and it was just what you and I s-said love would be like . . . o-only much, much more . . . wonderful!"

"Who was it? Tell me," Torilla begged.

"Can you not guess?" Beryl asked, half-smiling through her tears.

Torilla looked at her and suddenly she knew the answer.

"It was Rodney!"

Beryl nodded.

"Yes, Rodney. I suppose I was in . . . love with him ever since I was a child . . . but I did not . . . understand that it was love . . . not until he was . . . going away to j-join his Regiment."

"I remember that," Torilla said in a low voice, "but I never realised . . ."

"Aunt Elizabeth had just died, and you were . . . too unhappy to pay much attention to m-me. I intended to t-tell you, but both Rodney and I were so afraid that if anyone guessed we were in l-love with each other he would be forbidden the house."

She looked at Torilla through her tears as she went on:

"You know neither Papa nor Mama would have thought him g-good enough for me."

She gave a little sob and once again her hands went up to her face.

"Good enough!" she said in a muffled voice. "He

was ... everything I ever wanted and he t-told me that he loved me more than l-life itself."

Her voice broke and now she was sobbing un-controllably. Torilla could only hold her close, the tears running down her own face.

"You will not remember," Beryl went on after a little while, "but I went to London for a few days, telling Papa I was going to stay with Mama ... but she did not know I had left the Hall. Rodney and I were ... married by ... Special Licence. We went to an Hotel together and ... Torilla ... it was then I found what Heaven is ... really like!"

"I understand," Torilla murmured.

"It was so ... wonderful, so marvellous," Beryl said. "Then Rodney had to say good-bye because his Regiment was sailing for Spain."

Torilla remembered that Rodney had been part of the Division that was sent out early in 1814 to reen-force the Duke of Wellington's armies in his drive through Spain to France.

"Rodney was quite certain," Beryl went on, "that the war would not last long. When he returned we were going to tell Papa that we were married. Then there would have been ... nothing they could do about it ... but he never came ... back."

Beryl was crying again and Torilla murmured endearments as she cried too.

With an effort Beryl continued:

"I ... I have ... never told anyone ... what I have ... told you now ... there was ... no point in anyone ... knowing, once Rodney was ... killed."

"Not even the ... Marquis?"

"What would be the point?" Beryl asked, wiping the tears from her face.

"You do not think he has a ... right to know?"

"I do not enquire about Gallen's past and I shall not expect him to question me about mine."

Beryl looked in the mirror and saw Torilla's head reflected beside her own and the tears on her cheeks.

"Do not worry about me, dearest," she said. "It is the last time I shall cry about Rodney . . . the last time I shall speak of him. It is all over and done with."

"But you cannot forget," Torilla said softly.

"I shall try," Beryl said in a firm voice. "I shall try never to think of him again."

Torilla rose from her knees to stand looking down at the pink wedding-gown lying on the bed.

It was so like Beryl, she thought, in some strange way, to be honest enough with herself not to wear a white gown.

She thought now how blind she must have been not to realise that Rodney and Beryl always had a special feeling for each other.

Looking back, she could remember a thousand incidents that might have given her a clue to the fact that they loved each other in a different way from how they loved her.

She had been two years younger than Beryl and five years younger than Rodney and she had therefore looked at them with the eyes of a child.

Only now because she loved the Marquis could she understand why when they were together there was an inescapable magnetism in the air, and when they looked into each other's eyes it had been hard to look away.

Now so many things that she had not understood where Beryl was concerned were made clear.

Because she had lost the one thing that mattered in her life, she had plunged into the world of social gaiety in an effort to forget.

She sought admiration, she sought the love she had lost, even while she knew she would never find it again.

And so while she could not be satisfied in love, she would try to replace it with ambition, and she had achieved that when the Marquis asked her to marry him.

It was all very clear, Torilla thought, and she

knew that this was a further reason why she could do nothing to take the Marquis from her.

Beryl had lost Rodney, who was the love of her life, and a great Social position was her only substitute.

"At least my wearing pink will give them something to talk about," Beryl said in a voice which told Torilla that she had once again assumed the mask which hid her real feelings.

"It might make them . . . speculate why you are . . . wearing it," Torilla said hesitatingly.

"They will do that whatever I wear," Beryl replied. "You do not suppose that those gossiping old chatterboxes have not paired me off with innumerable lovers by this time? Charles Newall is only the latest."

She gave a pathetic little laugh that was not far from tears, and went on:

"There were several men last year whom they whispered about in corners and as many the year before."

"And you do not . . . mind?" Torilla asked.

"Why should I?" Beryl replied, shrugging her shoulders. "It is better to be talked about than ignored, and I should hate—really hate—no-one to notice me."

She saw the expression on Torilla's face and rose from the stool to come to her side.

"I am glad I have told you my secret, dearest," she said. "You are the only person who would understand; the only person who will know why sometimes I do outrageous things just to . . . forget."

"I do understand," Torilla said. "But, Beryl, remember that because he loved you Rodney will always be near you as I feel Mama near me."

Beryl stiffened.

"I have tried to believe that," she said. "When I first learnt that he was dead I used to cry out to him in the darkness to come to me, to hold me in his arms as he did when he was alive, but he . . . never came."

Her voice hardened as she went on:

"I told myself then that all the stories of an

after-life that your father talks about so glibly were a lot of nonsense. When someone dies there is only hell for those who are left behind."

"No, no!" Torilla said. "You must not think that! I have often felt when I have been desperately unhappy that Mama was near me. I know there is no death."

"Then why does Rodney not come to me?" Beryl asked. "He loved me, Torilla, as no-one will ever love me again. We belonged to each other, and yet now he is apparently content to leave me . . . alone."

"I do not believe that," Torilla said.

"Well, I do!" Beryl answered.

Once again there were tears in her eyes and she wiped them away.

"We cannot go out now, seeing what a freak I have made of myself. I am going to lie down, Torilla, and I suggest you do the same. There is a dinner-party tonight, but only a small one."

"You had better not stay up late, since you are being married tomorrow," Torilla replied, trying to speak naturally.

"I suppose not," Beryl agreed. "Gallen is not coming to dinner, I cannot think why. He sent his apologies this morning and said he has made other plans."

She smiled mockingly as she added:

"I expect he plans to say good-bye to one of his flirts. I wonder if it is the widow with whom he was so enamoured at one time, or a very delectable red-head I saw him with one night at a Theatre?"

Torilla was quite certain it was neither of these women, and what the Marquis was really avoiding was a small, intimate dinner-party at which she would be present.

'I should have gone north before the wedding,' she thought, but it had been impossible to leave Beryl and now in fact she was glad she had not done so.

She felt that in some way it had been a relief for Beryl to tell her the truth, and it swept away much of the anxiety she had felt about her cousin's character having altered since she had been such a success in London.

It hurt her to think of Beryl's unhappiness hidden beneath all the froth and gaiety of the Social World.

But at least Beryl had been married to Rodney; she had known the unutterable bliss of being his wife; they had had, as Beryl had said herself, three days of Heaven.

When Torilla went back to Barrowfield there would be only the memory of one wonderful kiss and the touch of the Marquis's fingers on her wrist.

That was all she had to last her for the rest of her life.

Yet because she loved him so deeply, he would always be in her thoughts.

Whatever physically he might mean to Beryl, or to any other woman, spiritually he would remain hers for all eternity.

*   *   *

There was so much commotion and fuss on the morning of the wedding that Torilla felt they would never reach the Church.

The Countess was rushing round the house, giving the servants orders, then countermanding them, and the confusion was increased by the late arrival of the Earl.

His carriage had been delayed on the road and at one moment they thought he must have forgotten the day and would not be there to give the bride away.

Combined with all this there was a constant stream of callers bringing notes and messages and belated presents. Florists delivering bouquets and dressmakers bringing items of clothing which had needed last-minute alterations.

There were a dozen trunks to be packed for Beryl's honeymoon.

Again, either the Countess or Beryl kept changing their minds as to what was to be included and what was to be sent to the Marquis's Castle in Huntingdon-shire.

The only person not particularly involved was Torilla herself.

Although she tried to keep close to her cousin in case she should need her, Beryl was in one of her moods when she was ready to think everything amusing and take nothing seriously.

She infuriated the Earl by telling him that his smart London coat was too tight for him, and when she tried to change her mother's hat the Countess screamed at her in exasperation.

"Do not interfere, Beryl!" she stormed. "Leave me alone and look after your own things. I am quite certain that you and your maid have forgotten half the gowns that should have been packed."

"If so, I will buy some more," Beryl retorted tartly.

Finally she was dressed in the pink gown which had evoked a storm of opposition both from her father and her mother.

"Pink? Who ever heard of a bride wearing pink?" they asked, for once both being in accord.

"It is extremely unconventional," the Earl said pompously.

"I have no wish to be a conventional bride," Beryl replied, "and you know as well as I do, Papa, that I am looking very beautiful and everyone will tell you so."

"Why did you not consult me and ask my advice?" the Countess asked over and over again. "It is a great mistake for the bride not to follow tradition."

"Well, it is too late now," Beryl answered. "Either I come to the Church in pink or you can call the wedding off. Perhaps Gallen will be quite relieved."

As the Earl and Countess had no desire to lose such an important son-in-law, they were silenced by Beryl's suggestion, and eventually, only a few minutes late on schedule, the Countess and Torilla left for the

Church, leaving Beryl and her father to follow in another carriage.

"I only hope Gallen will know how to deal with Beryl," the Countess said sharply as they set off. "I find her extremely annoying at times."

"She looks very beautiful, Aunt Louise," Torilla said soothingly.

But nothing would placate her aunt, who muttered and grumbled all the way to the Church.

Her efforts for Beryl's sake to get the Countess into a good humour prevented Torilla from being conscious of her own feelings.

She had not slept last night, but had lain awake wrestling with her conscience and tempted by what she felt were all the devils in hell.

Once she actually rose from her bed, lit a candle, and started a note to the Marquis:

> *I love You. I cannot face the future without*
> *You. I will do as You asked and . . .*

She stopped, stared down at what she had written, and knew it was wicked and the prompting of evil.

Frantically she tore the note into tiny pieces, then flung herself on the bed, crying desperately, despairingly, until she could cry no more.

When in the Church she saw the Marquis come from the Vestry to stand waiting at the Chancel steps for his bride, she felt as if a dark cloud encompassed her.

How could she endure the years ahead without him? How could obedience to duty or honour compensate either of them for an empty, barren existence without love?

As Torilla with her eyes downcast followed Beryl up the aisle, walking a few feet behind her glittering rose-covered train, she felt that her whole body was one dull ache and the agony in her breast was unbearable.

'I love him! I love him!'

She had the same overwhelming desire that she had felt last night to run to his side and tell him that she was ready to go with him anywhere in the world so long as they could be together.

The Bishop, wearing his mitre and full vestments, began the Service and Torilla raising her eyes saw that the Marquis was standing beside Beryl.

She looked at his broad shoulders, the outline of his dark head, and knew that his face would be set and grim, the lines deeply etched.

She heard the Bishop say:

"Therefore, if any man can show any just cause why these two people may not lawfully be joined together, let him now speak or hereafter hold his peace."

"A just cause!" Torilla repeated beneath her breath.

What was more just than love? What was more important in marriage than that two people who were to be man and wife should love each other with their hearts and souls as she loved the Marquis?

She wanted to cry out and stop the wedding, but after the little pause which followed the Bishop's words he continued:

"I require and charge you both, that as you will answer at the dreadful day of judgement when the secrets of all hearts shall be disclosed, that if either of you know of any just impediment why ye may not be lawfully joined together in matrimony ye now confess it."

Torilla felt as if the Marquis was reaching out to her, telling her that she already knew the secrets within his heart.

Her eyes were still on the back of his head and she almost expected him to turn round and look at her. The Bishop continued:

"Gallen Alexander, will you take this woman to be your wedded wife, to live together after God's holy ordinance . . ."

The congregation in their silks and satins seemed to move dizzily round her and Torilla thought she was going to faint.

Suddenly from the back of the Church a voice rang out.

"Stop this marriage! It must not take place!"

Every head turned and startled Torilla turned too.

Standing in the aisle just inside the west door there was a man, but because he had his back to the light she could not see his face.

He was tall, but as he came walking up the aisle she saw that he limped and his riding-boots were covered in dust.

Then as he came a few steps nearer she saw there was the gash of a deep but healed wound on the man's forehead and at that moment she recognised him!

At the cry from the end of the Church the Bishop had stopped reading the Service and both Beryl and the Marquis had slowly turned round.

Now there was a scream which echoed high into the roof, a scream that was followed by the incredulous cry of "Rodney!"

Beryl was running down the aisle, stumbling over her train and only being prevented from falling by Rodney catching her in his arms.

"Rodney . . . Rodney! You are . . . alive! You are . . . alive!"

The words were so incoherent and yet so poignant with an inexpressible joy that they brought tears to the eyes of every women in the congregation.

"You were . . . dead! But you are . . . alive . . . alive!" Beryl went on. "Oh, Rodney! Rodney!"

"I am alive, my precious wife," Rodney said, "and I cannot allow you to marry anyone else."

"As if I would . . . want to!" Beryl answered. "Oh, darling, I have been so . . . miserable . . . so broken-hearted. I thought never to . . . see you . . . again!"

Her voice broke on the last word and anyway it would have been impossible to say more, for Rodney was kissing her, kissing her passionately, quite regardless of the staring eyes of everyone round them.

* * *

Torilla could never remember afterwards how they got from St. George's, Hanover Square, to Carlton House.

Actually she travelled in the same carriage as the Earl and Countess, who were too stunned to do anything but just murmur Rodney's name over and over again.

He had explained who he was to the Bishop before they left.

He told His Grace briefly that he had only just arrived from France and had ridden all night to reach the Church in time to prevent Beryl from committing bigamy.

At Carlton House he had apologised to the Prince Regent for his appearance, but the Prince, intrigued by the story, had waved such unimportant matters aside.

"You must tell me, my dear boy, exactly what happened," he said in his thick plummy voice. "How is it possible that you were overlooked when our armies left France?"

What she did not hear at the Reception, Torilla learnt later when they all went back to Curzon House.

After the battle of Toulouse, where Rodney had been severely wounded and left on the battlefield for dead, he had been stripped of his uniform.

The scavengers who were a menace on every battlefield took everything he possessed, even down to his boots.

The wound in his head had left him completely unconscious and he also had a bullet in his leg.

He had apparently been overlooked by the British when they collected their casualties, and it was only when two Catholic Priests were reading the

Burial-Service over the dead that they found he was alive.

They had taken him to a Convent where the nuns were caring for a number of wounded who were too ill to be moved to the Hospitals in Toulouse or Bordeaux.

They had at first, Rodney related, thought it would be impossible to save his life, but when gradually after some months he could think and speak he found he had lost his memory.

"I had not the slightest idea of my name, or even that I was English," he said.

"And you did not remember me?" Beryl asked.

He had his arms round her as he told them the story.

Now he looked down at her with an expression of love in his eyes which made Torilla know that her cousin's happiness was assured for all time.

"You were, my darling, the first person I remembered, and when I came back to sanity," he said, "I saw your lovely face very clearly, but your name escaped me."

"It is the . . . same as . . . yours," Beryl said with a little sob.

"I only knew that later," Rodney answered, and kissed her forehead.

"Go on!" the Countess begged. "I must hear the end of the story."

"It was only three weeks ago," Rodney said, "that suddenly something which must have blocked my mind cleared and I remembered everything! I awoke one morning to know my name, my Regiment, and who was my wife!"

His arms tightened round Beryl as he went on:

"I knew then that the only thing that mattered was that I should get back to you, my precious."

"Why did it take you so long?"

"To begin with, as I had no money, I had to get to Paris," Rodney replied. "I knew that the British Embassy would help me, and I was not mistaken. Our

Ambassador believed the story I had to tell and paid my fare back to England."

"And quite right, too," the Earl remarked.

"When I reached Dover I bought an English newspaper to see what had been happening here," Rodney went on, "and almost the first thing I read was the report that my wife was to be married the following day."

"Oh, darling, were you . . . horrified?" Beryl questioned.

"I was determined to stop the wedding," Rodney said firmly, "and I have succeeded."

"You are not . . . angry," she asked in a very small voice, "that I should have agreed to . . . marry someone . . . else?"

She had forgotten, Torilla realised, that there was anyone else present and she was speaking to Rodney as if they were alone on a magical island.

And that in fact was where they were, she thought, alone and together and what was outside the circle of their happiness was of no significance.

There was so much more to hear, but Rodney was quite positive in what he wished to do.

"I want a bath, my darling," he said to Beryl, "and afterwards I would like to rest. Tomorrow morning early we will go home."

He saw the question in her eyes and added:

"I would not want my mother to suffer any longer."

"No, of course not," Beryl agreed, "and I want to see your mother and father's happiness when you walk into the house after they have mourned you for so long."

Everything was arranged just as Rodney wanted it, and Torilla knew that that was exactly how Beryl's life would run in the future.

Because she loved Rodney he would always be her Master.

The Social World had seen the last of the "Incomparable," the girl who had Social ambitions, and who wanted to be an important hostess covered in diamonds.

All Beryl would want in the future was to be with Rodney and together they had the only thing which really mattered—their love.

Chapter Seven

The Stage-Coach trundled down the Great North Road, stopping at every village and crossroads.

It had left London at seven o'clock from the Lamb at Islington, and Torilla knew they would be stopping soon at Baldock for the passengers to have a light repast.

She was almost oblivious to the discomfort of sitting squashed between two countrywomen and hardly noticed that a small boy was dropping pieces of chocolate on her muslin gown.

Deep in her thoughts, she had only aroused herself when the Coach reached Hatfield to think of Beryl and Rodney, and she knew how happy they must be together.

She had not left London immediately after the interrupted wedding, as she had meant to do, because the Earl had hurried back to Hertfordshire and her aunt had looked rather helplessly at the huge collection of presents.

"These will all have to go back," she said, "and although the servants can pack them up I will have to find the addresses of the senders."

"I will help you, Aunt Louise," Torilla said, and for once the Countess seemed grateful for her assistance.

They worked hard for the next three days and

when only a few anonymous parcels remained without
addresses, the Countess said:

"I only hope some of our so-called friends will
have the graciousness to return these gifts to Beryl and
—Rodney."

There was a note in her voice which told Torilla
all too clearly how deeply her aunt regretted that
Beryl had not made the brilliant Social Marriage for
which she had hoped.

"Beryl is very happy, Aunt Louise," she said, and
it was in fact an assurance she had repeated a dozen
times already.

"She had so many chances," the Countess replied, "but Rodney Marsden . . . !"

It was unnecessary for her to say more. Then as
if a thought suddenly struck her the Countess said
briskly:

"Now I have time to think about you, Torilla,
and I am sure Lord Arkley has not forgotten you. We
must ask him to dinner."

Torilla had risen to her feet.

"I must go back to Papa, Aunt Louise. He is . . .
expecting me."

The Countess considered for a moment.

"Perhaps Lord Arkley, like everyone else, will
have left London now that the Prince has gone to
Brighton."

She looked at Torilla as if appraising her looks,
then she added:

"Go to your father now if you wish, but I will
write to him and invite you to stay in September. Then,
Torilla, I will entertain for you."

Torilla realised that her aunt was transferring her
ambitions for Beryl to herself, but she knew it was
hopeless to say that she had no intention of marrying
anyone other than one person—and he had disappeared!

She had half-expected, although she thought it
might prove impossible, that the Marquis would send

her a note or possibly a verbal message after Rodney had stopped the wedding. But the Marquis had become invisible.

He had not gone on to Carlton House, which was understandable, but no-one had heard anything of him since, and now, sitting in the Stage-Coach, Torilla could not help wondering if perhaps he felt humiliated by what had occurred.

Certainly it had given the gossips something to snigger about and Torilla was sure that it was the main topic of conversation from St. James's Street to Chelsea.

Up to the last moment of leaving London she had wondered and hoped, but there had been nothing for her except two letters from Barrowfield, the first being from her father.

His letter was ecstatic with a happiness she had not seen in him since her mother died.

Buddle Air-Pumps were being installed in the pit, new machinery introduced to remove the water, the props had all been reenforced or replaced, Davy Safety-Lamps were provided, and the miners themselves could hardly believe the difference that increased wages had made in their lives.

It was left, however, for Abby to tell Torilla that her father was in much better health than when she had left Barrowfield. Abby wrote:

> *The Master's putting on weight, which is due
> to the fact that he is no longer so worried
> about the sick and needy. The Relief Fund
> which His Lordship set up has lifted from
> him the care of the children, the crippled,
> and the very old. But them Coxwolds, of
> course, are still getting more than their fair
> share!*

Torilla had laughed, knowing how much Abby resented the manner in which the Coxwolds extorted money from her father, then went on reading:

*I expect you know His Lordship's doubled
the Master's stipend and now I've got two
young girls to help me in the house and the
food is like your dear Mother used to order
when we lived in Hertfordshire.*

Torilla had given a little sigh of satisfaction. Then
she asked herself, as she had so often done before,
whether any man could be so wonderful, so kind, or
so generous as the Marquis had been.

'I want to thank him,' she thought, and wondered
almost despairingly whether she would ever have the
opportunity.

The Stage-Coach drew up outside the Royal
George and the passengers hurriedly climbed out.

"Twenty minutes, ladies and gent'men!" the
guard said, and everyone rushed into the Inn, determined to be served first.

It was only as she alighted, carrying her small
valise, that Torilla realised the mess the child had made
of her gown, and that after sitting for so long she felt
hot and uncomfortable.

Inside the Inn, she asked a chambermaid if there
was a room in which she could change, and was taken
upstairs to a bed-chamber that was not in use.

Torilla did not hurry. She knew that the food
would not be very appetising and she was, in fact,
not hungry.

She washed in cold water, then taking from her
valise a fresh gown which she had intended to put on
for supper that evening, she took off the one which
showed all too clearly the imprint of chocolate-covered
fingers.

She tidied her hair in the mirror and saw her
eyes wide and worried and with a suspicion of sadness
in their depths looking back at her.

"Perhaps he does not . . . want me any . . . more?"
she questioned, and turned away because it was an
agony even to imagine such a thing.

It was so hot that she did not put on her bonnet, but carrying it with her valise she went downstairs again.

There would only be time now, she thought, to ask for a cup of tea.

As she reached the bottom of the stairs she found the landlord waiting for her.

"This way, please, Madam," he said.

She put down her valise, thinking she would pick it up when she came from the Coffee-Room.

The landlord opened a door and she walked in.

Only when she was inside did she realise that she was in an empty room except for one person standing at the far end of it.

He turned to face her and for a moment neither of them could move.

Without speaking the Marquis held out his arms and she ran towards him like a homing pigeon. He held her so tightly that it was hard to breathe.

As Torilla raised her eyes to his he looked down into them and she thought the whole room was suddenly lit by a thousand candles.

Then he was kissing her wildly, frantically, passionately, as if they had stood on the brink of disaster and yet by some miracle had been saved from destruction.

It was as marvellous and divine as the kiss he had given her before, but now it was more intense, more poignant, and she knew that her love was a force that had grown so strong that it was like a tempestuous sea or a burning fire.

"I love you! I love you!" she wanted to cry.

But the Marquis's lips drew her heart from her body and made it his and there was nothing in the world but him and he was love itself.

Only after a long, long time did he raise his head to say in a voice deep and unsteady:

"My precious, my little love, I thought I had lost you."

"Oh, Gallen!"

She hid her face as she spoke against his shoulder and the tears were running down her face from sheer happiness.

"It is all right, my darling," the Marquis said. "It is all over."

He kissed her hair as he added:

"I am so grateful, so unspeakably grateful, that the agony is past and we can be together."

"To . . . gether . . ."

Torilla echoed the words through her tears.

Then he kissed her again, a long, slow, possessive kiss which made her feel as if her whole body melted into his. . . .

Some time later they sat at a small table and ate and drank, although what it was Torilla had no idea.

She could only look at the Marquis and feel that she was held captive by the expression in his eyes.

She had not known it could be possible for him to look so young, so happy, so carefree. The lines of cynicism were gone and there was a radiance in his face which she knew was echoed by hers.

It was difficult even to speak. They could only look at each other and feel as if they had died and been reborn.

Once Torilla put out her hand to touch the Marquis.

"You are really . . . there?" she asked.

"That is what I want to say to you, my wonderful, beautiful, perfect little love."

When the meal was over the Marquis drew Torilla to her feet and holding her by the hand walked from the private room along the passage to the yard.

She saw that his Phaeton was waiting there, drawn by the superb chestnut horses which she had learnt when she was at the Peligan belonged to him.

Now there was no groom; only the ostlers from the Inn were at the horses' heads.

Torilla tied the ribbons of her bonnet under her chin and only as she did so did she exclaim:

"My luggage! It was on the Stage-Coach."

The Marquis smiled.

"My servants have already taken it on ahead of us."

He helped Torilla up into the Phaeton, climbed up himself, threw two golden guineas to the delighted ostlers, and then they were off, bowling at a tremendous speed along the road leading north.

Only when they were clear of the houses and out in the green countryside did Torilla ask:

"Where are we going?"

"First to visit my mother," the Marquis replied. "I must tell you she is absolutely convinced it was her prayers alone which brought Rodney Marsden back from the grave and saved me from a loveless marriage."

Torilla turned her head to look at him and he went on:

"I expect you realised that after I was saved by fate or prayer I left London immediately to take my mother home."

"I did not ... think of your doing ... that," Torilla said in a low voice.

The Marquis looked surprised.

"Then what did you imagine had happened to me, my darling?"

There was a pause before Torilla said hesitatingly:

"I ... thought perhaps you did not ... want me any more."

"I will tell you how much I want you and need you," the Marquis replied, "tonight after we are married!"

She looked at him in a startled fashion as he said:

"You must realise, my precious heart, that we

have to be very circumspect and very secret about our wedding. I will not have you gossiped about."

"And we can really be . . . married tonight?"

Now Torilla's eyes were like stars and there was a note in her voice that made the Marquis say:

"If you look at me like that I shall be unable to drive carefully and we will have an accident!"

Torilla gave a little laugh of sheer happiness and moving closer to him laid her cheek against his arm.

"Can I really marry . . . you so . . . quickly?" she asked.

"It is all arranged," the Marquis answered. "We will be married in my own Chapel at the Castle by my Chaplain, and the only witness will be my mother. No-one will know anything about it for some months."

"It sounds too wonderful!" Torilla cried, and she knew the Marquis felt the same.

They drove along almost in silence until the Marquis drew his team to a standstill and she saw a little way to the left of them across a winding river the Castle set amid the green foliage of protective trees.

She had expected it to be impressive, but it looked enormous, its grey stone silver in the sunshine, the Marquis's flag flying from the highest tower.

He did not speak, but his eyes were on her face and after a moment Torilla said in a low voice:

"I shall not be a . . . brilliant Social Hostess."

"No?" the Marquis questioned.

"I shall not be . . . sophisticated or . . . witty."

"No?" he said again.

She looked up at him, her eyes suddenly troubled.

"I have . . . nothing to give you but . . . love."

He held the reins in one hand and put his arm round her.

"Do you think I want anything else?" he asked, his voice deep and passionate.

His lips touched hers and she felt his fiery desire on them. Then he whipped up his horses and they moved off at a pace which told her he was impatient for what lay ahead.

They went first to the Dower House which lay at the far end of the Park which surrounded the Castle.

Grooms appeared to run to the horses' heads and the Marquis helped Torilla down and led her into the house.

For the first time she felt a little apprehensive at meeting the Marquis's mother.

Supposing she did not think her good enough for her son? Suppose she had other plans for him now that he was free again?

The Marquis opened a door and there sitting in the sunlight of the bow-window Torilla saw a grey-haired woman with a face that somehow reminded her of her own mother.

There was the same sweetness of expression, the same kindness in her eyes, the same smile of welcome.

The Dowager Marchioness was looking at her son and he said in a voice that was unmistakably proud:

"I have brought Torilla to meet you, Mama."

"I have been so greatly looking forward to this moment, dearest," the Dowager Marchioness replied, then she held out both hands to Torilla.

* * *

Torilla walked hand in hand with her husband in a garden that was brilliant with flowers. They filled the air with fragrance and formed an indescribably beautiful kaleidoscope of colour.

The sun was hot on their heads and it was a relief when the Marquis drew her under the shade of the trees which bordered the lawns.

A path wound its way through the silver beeches which had a fairy-like appearance about them. Then the wood grew thicker and the sun could only percolate through the branches above them in tiny patches of gold.

"Where are you taking me, darling?" Torilla asked.

Her voice had a caressing note in it so that every word she uttered seemed an endearment.

"To a very special place," the Marquis replied. "It is where Mama told me she and Papa used to rest in the afternoon when they were on their honeymoon."

The house where the Marquis and Torilla were staying had been given to them as a wedding-present by the Dowager Marchioness.

She had explained to Torilla why she had done so.

"My husband and I spent our honeymoon there," she said in her soft, sweet voice, "and we were so ideally happy that afterwards he bought it from the friends who had lent it to us, and we kept it as a special place where we could be alone."

There was a reminiscent look in her eyes as she went on:

"Whenever Gallen's father was tired or seemed to have so many important things to do that it encroached upon our time together, we used to go there alone."

She smiled before she continued:

"It is a place where we talked only of love and ourselves, and to me it will therefore always be the most wonderful place I have ever known."

The moment Torilla reached the house with the Marquis, she had known that it would mean as much in their lives as it had in his father and mother's.

Built of warm, welcoming red brick, it was a very old house with a garden that was a Paradise of beauty and the whole atmosphere seemed redolent with love.

They had stayed the first night after they were married at the Castle. Then they set off, the Marquis driving his magnificent chestnuts, on their honeymoon.

Every minute they were together was so wonderful that Torilla thought at the end of every day it would be impossible to love the Marquis more than she did already, only to find each morning that she had been mistaken.

Walking through the wood with him now, she knew there was no need to ask him if he was happy.

She had not thought it possible for anyone to look so different from what he had done before and in consequence even more handsome, more irresistibly attractive.

Suddenly ahead of them there was a deep forest pool with the water as green as the trees reflected in it.

There were golden flowers round it and water-lilies with their wax-like petals lying on flat, green leaves.

At the side of the pool there was a small arbour covered with roses and honeysuckle, in which Torilla found when they reached it there was a large comfortable couch with many cushions.

"This is lovely, and so cool away from the heat of the sun!" she exclaimed.

She sat down on the couch as she spoke and found that it extended so that she could raise her feet and lie back against the cushions.

The Marquis pulled off his tight-fitting coat and threw it on the ground. Then he stood at the edge of the pool, searching for the fish which swam beneath the leaves of the water-lilies.

He was wearing only a thin white lawn shirt and Torilla looked at his square shoulders and his body tapering down to his slim hips in their tight yellow pantaloons.

'No man could be more attractive,' she thought, 'and he is mine . . . all mine . . . as I am his.'

As if, as always, he knew what she was thinking, the Marquis turned to throw himself down on the couch beside her.

"What conclusions have you come to?" he asked.

Torilla gave a little laugh.

"I would not want to make you conceited."

"I am the most conceited and the proudest man in the world because you say you love me."

"It is not what I say . . . it is what I . . . feel. I love you with my heart . . . my mind . . . my soul . . . I am all yours."

"My darling little wife."

The Marquis's voice was moved and he took Torilla's hand in his and kissed it, his lips lingering on each finger and finally on the soft palm.

It was very quiet and still and there was only the sound of bees taking the pollen from the roses and the honeysuckle.

"No place could be more perfect!" Torilla murmured.

"That is what you are, my sweet," the Marquis answered. "Perfect in every way. Oh, my darling, I worship you! I think you are the only good woman I have ever known."

"You must not say that," Torilla protested, "and I am not good. You will never know how hard it was for me not to agree to what you asked, not to go away with you, because without you there was only darkness and utter loneliness."

"But you refused me," the Marquis said.

Torilla remembered the letter she had torn up in the middle of the night.

"I was very . . . very . . . tempted to change my . . . mind," she whispered.

"And yet you did not do so because you thought it would be wrong."

"But I . . . wanted you so . . . desperately."

"As I wanted you," the Marquis answered, "and yet I knew, deep in my heart, you would do what was right, because it would be impossible for you to do anything else."

"We have been so lucky, so very, very lucky," Torilla said, "and that is why, my wonderful husband, we must try to help other people to find happiness as we have found ours."

She paused to ask:

"You *are* happy?"

"Do I need to answer such a foolish question?" the Marquis replied.

Raising himself on his elbow, he looked down at her.

His eyes searched her face and after a moment she asked:

"Why are you . . . looking at me like . . . that?"

"I am trying to find out what makes you so different from every other woman I have ever known," he answered. "You are breathtakingly beautiful, my darling, but it is so much more than that."

He put out his hand as he spoke and with his finger traced the smooth oval of her forehead.

"Sound, wise little head," he said as if he spoke to himself.

Then he touched first one of her eye-brows, then the other.

"Like birds' wings," he murmured, "carrying a message for those who have ears to hear."

"What sort of message?" Torilla asked.

"Of inspiration, as you inspire me, of sympathy, and of course of hope."

"That is what I thought I had lost as I walked up the aisle behind Beryl."

"I was suffering the agonies of the damned," the Marquis said. "I knew I had no-one to blame but myself and the punishment fitted all the many crimes I had committed."

"What . . . crimes?"

"You will never know. They are all in the past. In the future I shall be a model of virtue, not that it will be difficult because I have no wish to be anything but what you want me to be."

"I adore you . . . just as . . . you are."

"How could I have guessed," he went on, "how could I have known that morning when I felt like a man leaving the condemned cell, that Rodney Mars-

den, and of course my mother's prayers, would come
to our rescue?"

Torilla gave a little cry.

"We must not think about it," she said. "Sometimes when I wake up in the night in your arms I am
afraid it is all a wonderful dream and I shall find myself back at Barrowfield with only the smell of coal-
dust and the darkness of the mine."

"All that is over," the Marquis said firmly. "We
have a lot to do, my precious, in going round my possessions—and there are quite a number of them—to
see that no-one is suffering unnecessarily, and there
are no more horrors of which I am in ignorance."

"We will do that," Torilla agreed. "Then we will
come back here and be alone together?"

It was a question rather than a statement and the
Marquis smiled very tenderly as he said:

"It will always be waiting for us, this house of
love, where every day, my darling, I learn things
about love which I never knew before."

"And you will . . . teach them to . . . me?" Torilla whispered.

"You may be quite sure of that," he replied.

"You do not . . . mind that I am very . . . ignorant
. . . of such things?"

"Do you think I would want you different?" the
Marquis asked almost fiercely. "Your innocence and
your purity are not only what I have always sought, I
also find them extremely exciting."

"You are so magnificent . . . you have done . . .
so much . . . suppose after a time . . . you tire . . . of
me?"

"We are one person, my lovely sweetheart. It
would be easier to lose an arm or a leg than to tear
you out of my heart."

"Oh, Gallen!"

It was a sigh of sheer happiness. The Marquis was
still looking down at her. His eyes held an expression
which no woman had ever seen before.

He ran his finger down her small, straight nose, then outlined first her top lip, then the bottom one. As he felt a little quiver go through her he asked:

"Does that excite you, my little love?"

"It always . . . excites me when you . . . touch me."

"What do you think it does to me?" the Marquis asked in a deep voice.

His fingers encircled the softness of her neck, then moved lower to her breast.

He felt Torilla's whole body move as if to hidden music, and her breath came fitfully between her lips.

Then his mouth came down on hers, blotting out thought.

ABOUT THE AUTHOR

BARBARA CARTLAND, the celebrated romantic author, historian, playwright, lecturer, political speaker and television personality, has now written over 150 books. Miss Cartland has had a number of historical books published and several biographical ones, including that of her brother, Major Ronald Cartland, who was the first Member of Parliament to be killed in the War. This book had a Foreword by Sir Winston Churchill.

In private life, Barbara Cartland, who is a Dame of the Order of St. John of Jerusalem, has fought for better conditions and salaries for Midwives and Nurses. As President of the Royal College of Midwives (Hertfordshire Branch), she has been invested with the first Badge of Office ever given in Great Britain, which was subscribed to by the Midwives themselves. She has also championed the cause for old people and founded the first Romany Gypsy Camp in the world.

Barbara Cartland is deeply interested in Vitamin Therapy and is President of the British National Association for Health.

Barbara Cartland

The world's bestselling author of romantic fiction. Her stories are always captivating tales of intrigue, adventure and love.

Barbara Cartland

The world's bestselling author of romantic fiction. Her stories are always captivating tales of intrigue, adventure and love.